# Sun and Wind

## A LEGEND OF JOSEPH OF ARIMATHEA

BY WILLIAM BOARDMAN

Scepter

*Sun and Wind* was originally published by Garth Publications, Manchester, England in 2000. Copyright William Boardman. This Scepter Publishers edition, with revisions, is published in 2007, copyright William Boardman.

Cover photo: A Converted British Family Sheltering a Christian Priest from the Persecution of the Druids, 1850 (oil on canvas), Hunt, William Holman (1827–1910) / Ashmolean Museum, University of Oxford, UK; / www.bridgeman.co.uk

Design and Illustrations by Carol Sawyer/Rose Design

ISBN-13: 978-1-59417-039-3
ISBN-10: 1-59417-039-8

Printed in the United States of America

# ᛥ Contents

# ⚛ Foreword

To read the novel *Sun and Wind* as a simple adventure story with a few bits of Christian piety thrown in would be to miss the basic meaning of the book.

The legend is a saga, a saga with a profound Christian message. It echoes the sheer drama of the titanic struggle to establish Christianity in a pagan world. The story of Joseph's life in Britain is a little cameo of the life of the early Christians.

When Joseph lands in Britain he does not fully understand Christianity, he only met Jesus a few times during the brief stays of Jesus in Jerusalem prior to his crucifixion.

Joseph has been given an important role: to establish Christ's kingdom in Britain. Britain at this time is a desolate swamp of wind, rain, and fog with only brief moments of sunlight.

Sun and wind and rain make things grow and, in establishing a living world by cooperating with nature, life pits itself against the forces that seek to destroy it. It echoes the first attempts by Joseph and his new-found friend and helper, Eleanor, to establish Christian life in Britain.

Joseph abandons "the Old Jerusalem" as he is forced to flee the city and in Britain, without fully realizing it, he tries to establish "a New Jerusalem" not founded on violence. We see in stark contrast the progress of the two cities, one ruled by violence and the desire for revenge, and the other struggling to overcome brute instinct in order to establish a new kind of kingdom.

The reader, as a witness to the drama unfolding in the book, is able to take almost a God's-eye-view of the events taking place. With historical hindsight the reader is able to see the consequences of decisions taken by Joseph and those first Christians, which affect us to the present day.

Britain is full of pagan myths and of strange gods. Joseph with the natural gifts of an astute businessman seeks to use these natural energies and false beliefs of the Celts in order to guide them to a new form of spiritual life. How he achieves this is the meat of the book. As it says in the beginning "Go with him and love him because Joseph can teach us how to love."

The book is a moving account of Joseph's life in Britain.

# ☙ The Legend

The legend of Joseph of Arimathea or the "Glastonbury Legend" is an old one. Early written evidence of it dates from 1191.

Joseph of Arimathea, who appears in the Gospel of St. John, was, according to the legend, related to the virgin Mary and had connections with Cornwall, trading in tin and lead.

On one or more of his trading voyages, he is said to have brought the young Jesus with him.

The legend says that they built, at Glastonbury, a church of woven willow branches plastered with mud: "the wattle church." The stone "Lady Chapel" built between 1274 and 1291 is said to record by its length the exact size of the original wattle church.

Joseph had to escape from Jerusalem, after giving his tomb for the burial of Christ because he had publicly identified himself with the followers of Christ. This identification was a brave act since the local authorities had condemned Christ as a rebel, alleging that he had claimed kingship in defiance of Roman authority. The popular legend, centered on Glastonbury, says that Joseph landed somewhere in Southwest Britain and was the first founder of Celtic Christianity.

He reputedly brought with him the chalice of the Last Supper, the Holy Grail, which Christ had used in celebrating the first Eucharist.

The legend also relates that Joseph planted his staff and that it flourished and flowered like the "Rod of Jesse." The Glastonbury Thorn (Crataegus praecox) flowers, even today, at Christmas as well as in spring. Only the grafts from it have this property; thorn grown from the seed revert to the ordinary type.

The novel *Sun and Wind* suggests that features of the legend have undergone distortions over time compared to the events which actually took place, and it seeks to give a more plausible account.

# ⚜ Prologue

This is a story, a legend, drifting like a beam of pale light through the ether of time, to the present. It is written in modern idiom.

I hope that you will cast your mind's eye back along this beam, which comes from the beginning. I say "beginning" with conviction.

Imagine this isle of Britain, a dense forest of hill and mountain: dense, impenetrable forest, dank swamp made impassable by bramble and thorn. Along its edges dwelt the British, small, hardy, dressed in skins for their outer garments as protection against the cold, the rain and the wind. There were dwellings of wooden huts gathered in small villages, some linked by paths through the forest, others by mountain track.

They lived at the edge of the seas, huge gray seas, sometimes swelling into enormous moving mountains, crashing against the rocks; and riding these mountains were the little boats: sometimes wood, sometimes skin, made waterproof by tallow. Little hollows clinging to these dynamic, wreathing hills, seeking shelter in the rocky inlets.

Surrounded by seas, invaded by terror: terror from times past—memories of past calamities, terror of an unknown future where death is at the fateful door, and terror of the present. Terror in the dark forbidding woods, inhabited by spirits, terror of storm, terror of the mountains with their strange sounds and, above all, terror of each other.

It is a country of rain, of wind, of long dark clouds, of gray days shrouded in mist and light rain. Occasionally the sun, winning against the gods of water, would humor the green, make it glisten and radiate in the sunshine, coaxing out the aroma of flowers peeping through the foliage with their delicate colors, the air filled with the sound of birds and insects. In its rocky bays the sea smiles and rests, its gentle rhythm, heaving in sleep, bathed in sunshine.

Into one of these inlets, a man landed, like some strange insect resting from its exertions on some woodland debris. It is here that our legend begins.

Do not look for proof of this legend but enter it and live the drama. It is the drama of always: the setting is different, but it is the same drama.

Go with him on his journey, feel with him, suffer with him, and above all love him, because he can teach us love.

Sun and Wind

# CHAPTER 1

## ⚕ Jerusalem

I t was a bright morning as usual; Joseph liked to get up early, with the dawn if possible, just in time to have some dried meat or fish with some warm freshly made bread and a glass of sour wine, sharp, that put the teeth on edge; then just a handful of fruit or figs while he thought about the work and the contracts to be made that day.

He loved the early morning, the chill in the air and the trickling sounds of the fountain in the inner courtyard.

His favorite chair and table had already been laid by Azim. He knew the routine—fresh bread, a choice of something salty or spicy, and one of his three favorite breakfast wines; no talking to disturb the peace and solitude of the morning. There will be plenty of time for that when the children awake, and the wife and mother voices her concerns of the day in a rising crescendo: scolds, gives instructions on dressing and washing, calls to the servants, and then with a gliding sweep down the staircase to seek the support and solace of her husband for the morning drama that has just occurred or is about to occur. A kiss for daddy and then another sweep into breakfast.

Azim liked the mornings. He had been Joseph's house servant. He had taught him all he knew about hunting for small birds and animals, about fishing and how to cut, clean, and preserve. He passed on his knowledge of plants with stories attached to each one and of their usefulness in the daily cycle of life. Azim was forty and had fought against the legions of Rome. He knew a fine horse and could ride and shoot with bow and arrow from the saddle, a skill taught to the Parthians from an early age.

That he wasn't a slave was thanks to Joseph's father. As he lay wounded, hiding from the foraging bands of Romans who had just killed his family and burned their house, he was spotted by Jonathan, Joseph's father, who had been organizing the supply train. A wounded sixteen year old did not, in Jonathan's mind, constitute a threat. He hid him in one of his supply carts and brought him back to Jerusalem.

As a boy Joseph had idolised Azim. Azim had all the physical prowess that Joseph lacked. Joseph was very clever, pushed to the utmost by his ambitious parents. He was also very sensitive and imaginative and as a result cowardly when it came to tests of bravery. He instantly could imagine everything that could go wrong in a situation, and the solid pressure of caution seemed to freeze the very marrow of his bones, lock his joints, and cause his muscles to tremble. He loved Azim's stories of battles, escapes, and adventure. He tried to copy his skills and admired the smiling patience of Azim who put up with his failures.

But Joseph made up for these lacks by his sharp brain and his skill at business. He could read the business wind and spot a good deal when it was still on the horizon. He far excelled his father in business while he shared his hatred for the Romans. Neither he nor his father ever became Roman citizens, even though it could be advantageous. They relied on their wits rather than on their lineage. They smiled, entertained, joked, bribed, made contacts, gathered accurate information, trained their agents well to report anything of interest, and kept close counsel within the family, trusting no one else. Azim was both family servant and courier, knowing everything but saying nothing. He knew their secrets and why they strove for wealth: to rid Israel of the Romans.

Wars need money, lots of it. Allies are costly and liable to be more troublesome after victory than before. Allies need future enemies to keep them occupied and off your own threshold when their useful purpose has been served.

"Azim, my granary man is coming today. Can you give him the breakdown of wheat available for sale? Just sell enough to keep the army happy. There has been a shortfall of grain in Egypt this year and with a bit of luck we can get the Lebanon market. Prices are going to soar. Ask Simon to buy three more ships before anyone else gets wind of the news and prices go up. Keep them on short haul journeys so they are ready when we need them. No long trips to Marsalla for lead ingots.

"Azim. . . . What has my wife been up to? She seems to be getting more affectionate and that makes me nervous. It's affecting the children. You know how Karen and Ruth don't get on. One calls the other podgy pig and the other calls her silly duck.

"Yesterday, one was advising the other on hairstyles. Something's up, Azim. Thank God it can't affect my baby son. He can't talk and so he is excused from the babble. Keep an eye open, Azim, and let me know if some change has happened. My wife has even started to get up early. Very strange. Well, I have to go. I have to make money."

Azim too had noticed a change. The quiet morning had been his pleasure, his consolation. Now, he was beginning to feel uneasy. He had always cooked the master's breakfast—the two of them had followed the old familiar routine for years: a careful selection of favorites the evening before, sometimes the preparation of a broth, which needed a fire to be lit (the dry wood put in the iron cooker with the charcoal the night before, so that the charcoal would light quickly) the wine for the morning and the bitter herbs served with the meat or the fleshy tender ones with the salt fish; the lovely smell of freshly baked hot bread—all carefully laid out in silence and then back to his favorite corner to plan the day himself while his master pondered and ate.

But now this noise, this domesticity, at such an ungodly hour: he sucked at his thin cheeks till he looked even more like a worried rat, his sharp eyes, healthy and clear, showing patches of light under his dark bushy eyebrows. How could this problem be overcome with respect? Her energy needed to be guided, like a horse, which causes too much trouble because it is over-willing.

"Horses, that's it! I'll pass her over to Assab." Assab looked after the stables.

Azim and Assab shared their love of horses. They always went together when it came to buying and selling a horse. They would exchange stories of tricks used in horse trading: (pepper up the anus of a horse just before the sale to make it young and frisky with feet pattering and bolt upright ears, pricking lower eyelids to fill out the eye sockets, even painted gums and teeth for the unwary. Horse day was fun with wry exchanges of humor as each sought to belittle the other gently about their respective knowledge of the trade.

It was their joy and secret, which everybody knew about, to have collected two racing chariots in their many deals; and, of course, new horses had to be tried out for speed and controllability. What could be better than a race between them, around part of the estate, with a slight wager to give interest? Joseph knew of these escapades, although he chose not to notice. The crack of the whips could be heard miles away. It was good to hear Azim laugh out loud. The years, the cares, and the loneliness seemed to slip from his shoulders with the chomp of the hooves on the sand and the hissing of the wheels skillfully held away from the opponent, but not far enough to give him any advantage on the corners.

"Two new horses, Master. I've tried them out. They seem all right."

"Very good Azim, I trust your judgment."

Nothing more. The sale and purchase registered in the log.

Now Assab was going to help him in something more delicate than horseflesh—woman-kind, just as skittish and a lot more unpredictable. It would be more natural if Assab were not aware of the plot. There is nothing worse than Assab's trying to be clever. He first changes his voice, and then he tries to change his accent, the change sending a signal clearer than a beacon and being visible from about the same distance.

"Mistress, may I have a word with you?"

"Yes, certainly Azim."

"Well you know how master Joseph has been frequently attending meetings of late in the center of Jerusalem.

"In those kinds of circles presentation matters. Well, Assab keeps his horses in tip-top condition, his grooming is excellent and the chariot is always without blemish. But mistress, I think he doesn't quite have an eye for presentation. You know the functions he attends, and maybe the furnishings need an extra eye for detail: the feminine touch.

"You know how the wives talk, and there isn't much they miss. I know your mornings are busy, but I do think it important."

"Why of course, Azim, good observation. I shall be with Assab every morning before my husband leaves to make sure of the details."

Rebecca was actually delighted to be found useful in some part of the morning chores. Her new resolution about getting up early to be helpful to her husband was meeting with that smile from him made with a bit of an effort. Her intuitive sensibility told her that her gushy enthusiasm was causing a tidal race at the wrong time of the morning.

This time of the morning required the tranquility of a bay at dawn, rather than the foam of activity of a tide at full flood.

She was glad to be useful; she would go to the stables to arrange the tapestries of the chariot, matching them with the harness and bridle. Sober colors for stately occasions, brighter for military—even now she was getting excited about the whole idea. She would set the fashion for horse-ware.

# CHAPTER 2

# The Meeting

"Azim! Can you have a horse ready for me this evening? Nothing ostentatious . . .

"I have a meeting with Jesus of Nazareth, a country boy, who has met with some success at preaching to the ordinary people. My agents have given a good account of him and I want to see him before he becomes infatuated with the city set. Good preachers sometimes let success go to their heads. City life is different from the homely tales of country folk."

"Master, his mother, already comes to the house here. She has been gathering some women about her and they have some meetings in the women's part of the house."

"Ah, metanoia."

"I beg your pardon, Master?"

"Nothing, Azim, it's Greek . . . change of heart . . . I was commenting on the changes in my wife and children."

"Oh, very good, sir."

"Greek."

"Clever race, sir. Iron discipline. More initiative than the Romans.

"Never would have been conquered if they had not been so divided. Too many solutions resulting in dissolution."

"Very good, Azim!," in a burst of enthusiasm. "I like it, I like it. . . !

"I am going to quote that in one of my speeches. I shall write it down in my phrase book . . . right now. I like it!"

Azim loved it, when he had made an intellectual point. It raised him for a moment above the physical.

For a brief moment it was as though he were taking council with the gods . . . and they were impressed.

Intellectual appreciation from his master made his day.

"The horse shall be ready at sunset, master. Do you need a torchbearer and a guard?"

"No, Azim. Have my own sword ready and a fast horse. Guards talk and, for the moment, I don't want it known that I've arranged a meeting with him. . . . He could be useful to us, Azim, but I want to know what he is like first. . . . Whether he is an impostor or not. The city will soon bring out his true colors, whether it's fame or idealism, which drives him.

"Personal ambition for glory can rot a man, Azim. Too many people use religion but do not serve it. I sometimes feel that even the Romans have a better respect for religion than some of our kind . . .

"Well, Azim, I have to go.

"I shall be back late, a quick bite to eat, change clothes, then leave. A brown jacket, Azim. Not too elaborate. He is not a respecter of attire, although I believe he likes things neat. He does things well, even in his own clothes, I hear. Clean, simple, neat, and tidy, Azim. That's muster for this evening."

Evening came and Joseph was a little flustered when he got back home. Meetings with the Sanhedrin had not gone well. Feathers were being ruffled, the Romans were making new demands on control of religious gatherings and some rigorists wanted to make a stand and cause trouble, just to put the Romans on the defensive.

Anyway, he changed quickly, gathered a few thoughts together on what he was going to say, and then left.

He was met at the inn by an excited group of men, simple men, impressed when people of social standing showed an interest in the new movement. Such attitudes tired him. He had seen the same cycle before. Excitement, enthusiasm, then difficulties and declining interest as the novelty wore off with both audience and actors. They took his horse and one of them held it for him in the courtyard, while some of the more senior accompanied him into one of the rooms at the back of the inn, reserved for meetings of a discrete nature. Curtains were drawn, and the general noise of the inn maintained privacy.

After preliminary introductions and greetings, Joseph turned to Jesus wondering how he could say things quickly without appearing rude or offhand.

He tried a standard trick on such occasions for bringing the problem out in the open; some opening words of praise.

"Dear Jesus. I am genuinely pleased to meet you. As you know God has blessed me with considerable wealth. Praise be to God and his Will.

"Now as you may appreciate, time means money to me. Please don't think me rude, but I have many things to say to you, and not much time to say them. I have tried to see you early before you start preaching in Jerusalem. I have come to try and help you . . .

"My agents tell me you have met with success in the countryside. I want to give you advice about the city and about city life, particularly life at the top of the social tree.

"I would like you to listen to what I have to say without interrupting. You may ask questions at the end if something isn't clear to you. Agreed? Good!"

Joseph paused for a moment and then turned, leaned forward, and taking hold of the hands of Jesus, said:

"There are four essential ingredients to power: money, the sword, a strong ideal that will persuade people to die for the cause, and a charismatic person who can co-ordinate all those elements and above all at the right moment, can seize the opportunity when it presents itself . . .

"Alexander had almost all those elements, but he didn't have the true religion and so he failed . . .

"His appeal to religion lacked truth. It was contrived by people who thought they knew power. They tried to create an earthly religion to consolidate power among the people, but they didn't have the inspiration from God . . .

"Man-made religions lack the one necessary thing: they don't last forever. They don't strike at the nature of things . . .

"Nor can they give man sufficiency . . . to meet all his aspirations. . . . They suit only some and not others. . . . Their ideals are not strong enough to withstand the rigors of the effort required for success.

"That is why we have survived as a nation in spite of the might of evil thrown against us. We have survived because of the Covenant of God. For no other reason . . .

"If you look for earthly reasons for our survival, you will fail. There is no earthly reason for our survival. . . . No other system has survived intact for so long.

"We have survived because our survival has been the will of God. His promise made to us. No other: Not our intelligence, not our skill, not our fighting prowess, but the hand of God has held us and protected us. We use our wits, and because of our effort God gives us his wisdom and protection. As long as we respect his covenant He will protect us . . .

"Now I have the wealth . . . but I don't have the charisma for leadership.

"I am looking for the sword that is strong enough to defeat the Romans.

"The Nazarene rebel group are an ill-disciplined rabble. They can cause trouble but they will never defeat the disciplined might of Rome . . .

"I have not found a suitable sword. . . . I am looking for the man of charisma, who can lead our people. . . . My search is why I have come to you. Are you going to provide the inspiration to our people that will direct our people to victory?

"You have no need to answer that. . . . Time will give the answer for us. . . . A man has to be measured by results, not by verbal promises.

"Now, I have one thing to ask of you, go about your preaching to ordinary people and raise their hopes, but don't take on the Sanhedrin, and certainly not the Roman authorities, without asking my advice.

"You are not dealing here with county bumpkins, but with highly sophisticated and intelligent people. . . . They have military power. They have wealth and above all they are prepared to kill to get what they want.

"Now this latter point makes the rules of debate somewhat one-sided. . . . You will have to be extremely clever to achieve what you want. If you are unwise, you will lose everything, including your own head.

"Politics is the art of the achievable. Don't get too ambitious, especially in the beginning, and be ambivalent if necessary. Don't make your intentions clear, if the time is not opportune . . .

"For instance, my agents have reported, fairly accurately I think, about your stories to the people, good simple stories about shepherds and fishermen. Well, remember, your stories may be good for the ordinary Israelite, but the city Jews despise the ordinary Jew, the Am-ha-rez, because they are largely ignorant of the law . . .

"These stories will not make much impact here. . . . You might as well talk to the stones of the Temple. . . . God, I am sure, will hear you. . . . Nobody else will . . .

As a true Israelite who preaches the word of God sincerely, I know you must hate the Romans, as I do, and dream of the day when we shall be free.

"I am willing to sacrifice all my wealth—even my family, and I love them dearly—for the cause of the Lord and the progress of his religion, to make this land free and able to fulfill the Messianic promise made to us.

"And above all, Jesus, when you pray at night do it well. Many preachers use religion for a living, but they do not practice it. Many are corrupt. Corruption and the external practice of religion

is an odious combination, and such people are extremely dangerous. They carry within them the sulphurous smell of Lucifer.

"Well now. I must go. . . . It is not prudent for me to stay too
long. May I come again and talk to you?"

He said this because he meant it . . . he liked him.

Also, Joseph was thinking that when an important person
like himself asks an ordinary person like Jesus for permission,
then that ordinary person will be pleased by the request and so
will be less likely to be offended because the important person
had neglected to show the courtesy of eating with him.

"Of course, Joseph."

Joseph was a little perplexed by the amused kindly twinkle in
the eye.

"But I would like to ask one question."

"Yes, go ahead," said Joseph.

"Why does God permit evil and even at times allow it to
flourish?"

"That is a great mystery, my friend. I wish men knew the
answer. I often read the book of Job, over and over" said Joseph,
raising his finger. "We are being tested, Jesus. We are being tested
. . . and God will look on us with a kindly eye. Is that not sufficient for us? That the mighty God, creator of the universe, should
look on us kindly?"

The response was startling. Jesus arose swiftly took Joseph's
head in his hands, kissed him and then led him silently to the door.

"By the way, Jesus," Joseph turned remembering . . .

"Don't worry about your mother. She shall have the protection of my household. Go about your work, free from the fear
that she might be threatened and used as a lever on you to mod-
ify your actions. Some people are like that. I am pleased with her
influence on my wife and my two she-devil daughters. You may
use any of my resources in Jerusalem . . .

"Just say to any of my agents. . . . The master has need of it. I
shall instruct them to supply you at this request . . .

"Goodbye and thank you for receiving me."

Joseph went to his horse and rode out of the inn. a bit puzzled by the sudden reaction of affection. "A kindly man," he thought. "one capable of great friendship, I could be happy to be in his company, but he is not a leader. I think he would not have the ability to make the harsh decisions necessary for leadership, too homely; simple; capable of great personal affection; but not a leader. I think he cannot even ride a horse. . . . Who ever heard of a leader who can't ride a horse?

"I shall meet with him again soon," he decided.

Joseph did meet with Jesus again, on several occasions. Advising him, telling him about decisions of the Sanhedrin, warning him of plots, telling him not to stay in Jerusalem and not to tell people in advance about the places he intended to visit, warning him of assassination and telling him how to minimize risk by seeking the protection of the crowd.

He did not object to his attacks on the Sanhedrin. In fact he liked it.

"Country boy, rattling the high and mighty," he mused.

He always admired the plucky underdog.

# CHAPTER 3

## ⟡ The End (and Beginning)

The crucifixion came unexpectedly. The arrest was sudden: a late night call, a hurried meeting in the dead of night. Joseph was profoundly shocked at the use by Jesus of "the Sacred Words." Jesus had coolly called down his own death sentence. A man, claiming to be God.

The suddenness of the call in the middle of the night, the surprised shock at seeing Jesus in the hands of the Sanhedrin and the clear "blasphemy" of Jesus had stunned him into silence. He had abstained in the vote, as he wanted time to organize some defense. These trials always took a long time and so there was no point in doing anything hasty. He would hold his hand, appear calm and think out a plan in the morning. An accusation as big as this would take at least three to four months of legal debate and cross questioning: plenty of time to get up a good defense for Jesus.

He was outraged to find that events had been speedily concluded. No one at the trial had mentioned handing him over to the Romans. An initial condemnation was only a prelude to a long process . . . to prove that there was sufficient grounds for a case to be made against Jesus. Why the terrible rush for a speedy conclusion? It was insane.

He witnessed the scourging, the trial before Pilate, the masterful manipulation of the mob hired for the occasion.

He followed the crowd, staying with the Sanhedrin.

He waited until he died . . . and then went home.

Rebecca was waiting, anxious. "What happened?"

"He claimed to be God, Rebecca. He coldly, deliberately, slowly said 'the sacred words.'

"Oh, Rebecca! I have never seen such hatred; hatred that unhinges reason. They all did whatever they could to hurt and humiliate him and he did not say a word.

"Some of the Sanhedrin must have bribed the guards because I have never seen such a scourging. They must have wanted him to die under the lash. It was only the intervention of an officer which stopped the thrashing, saying that he had to appear before Pilate, and that it might go hard with them if he died before his trial.

"They called out the whole cohort, 750 men, in full uniform, just to mock him as King of the Jews? I have never seen such overreaction, such unreasoned hatred.

"His last words: 'My God, my God, why hast thou forsaken me?' were said with the metered rhythm of the Psalm. I was next to Caiphas, and I heard him gasp: 'Even now he is quoting from the psalms!'

"He looked at both of us, as he said it. Even then he was appealing to us.

"I believe him to be the Messiah, Rebecca. Some of our prophets have told us that the Messiah will be a suffering Messiah. A man of Sorrows. He allowed evil to do its worst. It was as though all the hidden hatred in men's hearts came out into the open and expressed itself on his body. They tried their worst. I have never seen such a frenzy of hatred . . . and he said not a word."

"Mary is with us, Joseph. She has asked us for help to bury her son."

"He shall have our grave, Rebecca, and may the Angel Raphael and Prophet Tobit help us."

"The Sanhedrin will not like it, Joseph."

"The Sanhedrin can go to hell!," Joseph shouted at the top of his voice.

"Jews condemning a Jew to die like that at the hands of the Romans! Unheard of!"

Joseph was trembling with anger. "I am going to gather my friends together and there is going to be a move of censure. Caiphas must go.

"The whole thing was arranged so carefully. . . . First the condemnation for heresy, but without anyone knowing the secret intention of condemning him to the Romans for crucifixion.

"A carefully arranged hidden agenda, pushed through by a prearranged plan, a quick vote with little discussion or delay, in the middle of the night, when everybody wants to go back home to bed.

"What careful planning! I have not seen an equal to such manipulation of the Sanhedrin and I have seen quite some political maneuverings before.

"No sane Jew would condemn another to such a humiliating death. Unless there is an insane hatred operating here. It's a hatred which has broken through the confines of loyalty to our nation and our Jewish brotherhood.

"Tell, Mary to leave it to me. I will arrange everything.

"He shall have a Jewish burial . . . in our family grave. I will deem it an honor."

# CHAPTER 4

## ᪥ A Court Hearing

Caiphas said: "I have requested this meeting of the temple court, concerning the Jesus business. There are still some matters outstanding.

"I have not invited Joseph. You probably know the reason. He has, of late, identified himself with a lost cause. This rather complicates matters. . . . Joseph and his wealth must be separated . . .

"Lost causes constitute no danger; Joseph without his wealth will constitute no danger.

"We can't have him turning against us and forming new alliances for our overthrow. We must strike first before he can use his money against us . . .

"While the conspiracy is still fresh in people's minds, we must conduct a cleaning up operation against leading conspirators," Caiphas continued.

"You can leave the country bumpkins; let them go back to their rabbit holes. It would be undignified for us to pursue them. Jews don't like Jews being handed over to the Romans. We cannot do that very often . . .

"We simply need to cut Joseph off from his wealth and he will be powerless.

"We need the Romans to complete the clean up. Pilate's secretary, Callistus, is willing, for a certain percentage of the proceeds; plus a certain percentage to Pilate; and the rest to us. We need the granaries; essential for any sustained hostilities . . .

"We were always counting on Joseph for supplies if the great day came. . . . Now we must manage without him."

After some discussion, with no one in favor of Joseph, the meeting ended.

Joseph, with the Romans against him, was a fallen star; no one with the slightest ambition would be identified with him.

It was agreed to confiscate his properties. The details were to be left to Callistus, since he had experience in the sequestration of the property of Rome's enemies and political opponents.

# CHAPTER 5

## ❧ Joseph's Anger

Rebecca was waiting for Joseph as he came down from an upper room.

"Joseph, Mary thanked you for your kindness. Some of the silly women are talking about having seen him. . . . Our servants, who helped prepare his body for burial are claiming to have seen him. They say they saw the wounds on his hands. Silly fools!"

"They are not silly, Rebecca. They're telling the truth."

"What do you mean, they're telling the truth?"

"They are telling the truth."

Joseph did not want to argue, nor did he want to go any further with the conversation. He was still trying to ponder the words that Jesus had said to him as he cradled his head with his scarred hands.

"We shall discuss it later."

With that Joseph abruptly left the house, to get out of the way. He went to work. He wanted to be alone and think things over.

He stopped on the way, to talk to some of his friends in business. He would use his financial muscle to bring down Caiphas, no matter how much it cost.

On his way to his dispatches office he called at the house of his chief agent, his cousin Reuben.

"I want you, Reuben, to update our dossier on Caiphas. I want everything about him and I shall pay handsomely for good information. . . . Caiphas must go, Reuben. He betrayed one of our own, to the death of a slave and without regard for our law. When you have finished show it to me and then make copies for the leading members of the Sanhedrin.

"When his treachery is made known, I shall show it to him and give him sufficient time to escape to the Persians. If he doesn't then I shall make a copy for the Romans. An eye for an eye and a tooth for a tooth. He betrayed our own to the Romans . . .

"By our law he should suffer the same . . . not more . . . not less . . . the same. . . . Yet," and here Joseph paused . . . "no crime is so bad as to condemn a Jew to the Romans for crucifixion.

"The punishment is disproportionate. He shall be spared that. We shall kill him rather than the Romans, if he becomes foolish and obstinate. I shall have my assassins ready.

"But, first, we must win over the Sanhedrin. We must expose the sins of Caiphas, make him a leper in the eyes of the Jews. Then cast him out . . .

"He must be cast out . . . into the desert . . . like the sacrificial goat. with his sins heaped upon him. . . . He must walk no more on the holy ground of Israel."

# CHAPTER 6

## ✢ A Meeting with Callistus

When he got to his work and to his dispatch room, Callistus was already waiting for him.

"Good morning, Joseph. You did quite a daring thing a few days ago: identifying yourself like that, in front of Pilate . . . with a rival to Roman leadership. . . . That crucifixion was an example of how we Romans deal with rival kings."

"That man was concerned with things of the spirit, not of politics, and you know it," replied Joseph quietly. "Whoever heard of a conqueror choosing to ride into a city on a donkey?"

"You condemned a man for paltry reasons in defiance of Roman law, which is the source of your power. What is going to happen to Rome if it continues to defy its own Law? You worship the gods of Law, but blaspheme against it when you choose to. What, under the gaze of all the gods, distinguishes you from the revolutionary who seeks to destroy the rule of your Law. . . . Only power, only power, the rule of might."

"Careful, my Jewish friend. This sounds like blasphemy against Pilate. Your Jewish leaders and ourselves have dealt with one blasphemer. Shall we have to deal with another?

"And, by the way, I am not well versed in your writings, but wasn't your Messiah supposed to come into Jerusalem . . . riding on a donkey? . . . Your Christ seems to have more of a sense of history than you, my friend.

"Romans are always suspicious of . . . innovators. Innovation is the enemy of good administration; it tends to upset the status quo: things like that mean turmoil and lots more administration. Innovation is the prerogative of Emperors, and rivals make for a lot of disturbance down below.

"Your Christ was an innovator and he is going to create quite some turmoil. He has awakened the aspirations of the poor and, my friend, that means turmoil. I think this little turmoil is not going to die down so nicely as people think . . .

"Well, I might as well get straight to the point: your family, all of them, have been arrested and should have been executed by now or soon will be. I don't believe in wasting time. I don't believe in slaves having a family. They pine too much and are unreliable.

"Pity you never became a Roman, Joseph. Conspirators, non-Roman, get very little leeway with Romans. At least their condemnation is swift without awkward cross-examinations.

"How I treat you will depend on your co-operation. I want to know all about your companies, so that I can do a full confiscation speedily. If you cheat me you shall find how a Roman treats a slave who tries to cheat him. If you cooperate I shall give you an administrative post in my household. You shall find it more to your taste than some other types of slave work . . .

"My guards are outside. We shall have to brand you and have you maimed. You will need to move around a little for your work and the temptation to escape will be great. They know what to do. I have given them my instructions."

Callistus got no further. He suddenly went silent, looking at Joseph.

Joseph looked at him, at his bulging eyes, which slowly closed. It was only then that he noticed the slim figure standing behind him and the thin silk cord around Callistus' neck.

"I cannot kill him, master, if I do the Romans will massacre the whole household. . . . Follow me."

Azim led Joseph down the side stairs on the outside of the house. Assab was holding the horses of both chariots. Joseph clambered aboard Azim's chariot and hung on as the chariots moved away slowly, so as not to attract attention. One went one way carrying a man servant and Assab . . . and the other Azim and Joseph, every head covered with a traveling cloth so that noone would recognize them.

Outside the city the whips cracked and Joseph's chariot made for the coast, the other, bearing Assab, went inland.

Assab would never know the destination of Azim.

Outside the city, Azim slowed the horses to preserve them for the long journey to the coast in the fierce heat.

They said nothing during the journey. Azim did not know what to say to console his Master and so remained silent. Joseph couldn't say anything. The last few days had been sheer madness and he couldn't absorb it all. He needed time and solitude. He needed to think things out, to adjust, to become oriented again, to get some balance back into his mind. He couldn't say anything with any meaning, and so he remained silent.

After some hours, Azim spoke.

"Master, we are going to an embarkation point, which we use when we want the Romans not to know what we're doing. I will speak to the captain of the ship. He knows it is best not to ask questions. They will not ask your name or anything about you . . .

I did not have time to get money. He will have to do it as a favor. The ship is going to Marsalla, taking rope and sail and tent cloth from Cilicia. From there, you will go by pack horse and donkey to Britain for lead and tin. You will not be returning with them. May God be with you, Joseph."

The shock of impending exile, made Joseph find his voice.

"Azim, what are you going to do?"

"Try to make it back to my people. . . . I need to return to get provisions without the Romans seeing me. Callistus didn't see me, and so he has no way to find out who attacked him. He doesn't know me and I may have time before somebody betrays me, to get what I need . . . and escape."

"Azim . . . go to Mary. She will help you. Her Son has conquered death. I don't know how. She will tell you what to do."
Almost in a daze, Joseph waited on the beach, boarded the
boat and sat among the ropes, while Azim negotiated with the
captain. They spoke in Phoenician. Azim left immediately when
the transaction was concluded afraid that even this momentary
pause would attract suspicion. He did not look back to say
farewell, fearful that this small gesture might cost Joseph his life.
Lying on the ropes in the hold out of sight, Joseph found he
couldn't cry. He wanted to cry, but couldn't. His insides seemed
like stone, his head numb. He didn't want to reflect. He just lay
and watched the wind catch the sails, the shadows of the clouds
scudding across the cloth, alternating with bright glare as the sun
broke out and cast fierce light onto the canvass.

"You will be cold tonight with only those silks on you and
that thin cloak," the wife of the captain called down to him. "I
shall make you a tunic out of the sailcloth of Cilicia, in exchange
for those clothes of yours. They will also help pay for your journey. The sailcloth will be more weather proof, but I warn you: this
cloth is so rough you will think you have been whipped by the
Romans. But it will be much better for the winds of the north.
You have not felt cold and damp properly until you have been to
Britain or at least they tell me so. We only go to Marsalla. You
will be able to get work at Marsalla, particularly if you can ride a
horse or handle a donkey."

And so it was. Joseph sat silent in the boat, alone with his
thoughts. He spoke to no one. He ate alone, slept on the cargo
and was left alone as the ship sailed the Mediterranean. Since it
was late spring, the ship sailed direct, only coming close to land to
seek bearings.

At Marsalla, he nodded his thanks to the captain and wife, as
he left the ship, following their directions to the market. He had
no money, and so the journey was pointless. He returned when
the animals had been loaded.

# CHAPTER 7

## ❧ The Journey

T he captain had already spoken to the train foreman. "Do you
prefer horses or donkeys?"

"Donkeys."

"Horses give more pay, and you don't have to walk."

"Donkeys."

"Donkeys it shall be. We leave at the third quarter. We need
to clear the town and prepare camp. Too many thieves know we
are here. You won't get much sleep tonight. We need all the
guards we can muster. The first few days will be hard until you get
used to it and your muscles get used to walking. Take plenty of
rope sandals or solea. I will deduct the cost from your pay later. I
will also lend you money for essential provisions. Pay me later
from your pay. You can get advice from any of the men. The Boss
also speaks Roman."

Joseph suffered greatly in those first days. His feet and his
legs were not used to walking. But gradually the regularity of the
work, the sun, wind, and rain, the day-long exercise, and simple
wholesome boiled wheat with a strong-smelling fish sauce and
sour wine gave strength to his limbs. Occasional fruit gathered on
the wayside gave him some comfort.

Each night they slept within the palisade surrounding the camps where they stopped. Joseph's feet hurt, he was not yet accustomed to the wooden soles of his solea. He soaked his feet every evening in strong salt and vinegar to harden them. He did not take off his solea at night hoping to hasten the breaking in process. And he did not remove his dagger, only his short sword, as he lay to sleep. Sleeping armed was advice he had received from Azim in one of his many tales.

The third night out was particularly hot and humid and Joseph could not sleep. His feet hurt terribly. He silently got out of his bedding and stretched his legs, leaning lightly against the palisade, as he massaged first one foot and then the other in the places where they were most painful. He wondered if his feet would allow him to continue the journey with the party. What would he do if he had to leave them? How could he survive? Joseph prayed.

Suddenly he found himself choking. A cord had been slipped around his neck and was being pulled tight. He arched his head back, momentarily, going in the direction of the pull and saw a gleaming set of teeth. He took out his dagger and pushed it between the teeth until it jarred against the back of the throat. Blood spattered his head, and the cord was released.

Joseph ran for his sword, yelling. He saw another hand over the palisade with a cord hanging from the hand. He slashed out and heard the yell.

Joseph shouted again; the thieves had chosen their time well: the early morning when sleep is deepest. There was a sentinel on watch. Joseph rushed to the gate, but he was already dead.

"Come on men," Joseph had remembered the shout of the foreman, the only British he knew. He started banging the cooking pots and utensils by the fire to simulate the sound of many men.

Slowly the sleepers realized what was happening and rushed for their weapons. It was some minutes before they assembled and began to scour the camp. They found no one, only two trails of blood.

In the morning they buried their companion without ceremony and surveyed the damage. Nothing had been stolen. The
horses had not panicked and bolted. This was considered almost
a miracle.

Joseph could not eat even though food was offered to him.
He had earned his companions respect, and they were grateful to
him. They all owed their lives to his prompt action. Joseph's
throat hurt and he found difficulty in swallowing. The night
episode had also drained the last of his courage. His legs gave way
and he felt he couldn't carry on. He had lost the will to walk.

Morvah, the leader of the pack train, knew the problem.
He, in his early days, had fought for his life against thieves and
experienced the same state of collapse afterwards.

To stab a man for the first time is not an easy thing to do, and
it has its effects.

Morvah ordered Joseph into one of the carts and told him to
lie down on top of the sailcloth. He gave him mead, which he
ordered him to drink. On an empty stomach the drink numbed
his senses; and he slept restlessly on the bumping cart, rolling
with the movement and jerking when the wheels passed over
stones. The movement calmed him and occupied his mind. Gradually Morvah gave him bits of dried meat and small pieces of
bread with the mead to bring back his appetite.

Joseph lay on the cart for two days and none of the men
complained. His feet also recovered and he was ready to resume
his duties.

Joseph did not weep until he got midway into Gaul. He lay
inside the camp palisade among the donkeys and the goods,
looking at the sky and the stars, off duty; and then the tears came,
flowing down the side of his face onto the leather bedding.

The next night he relived the terrors of the crucifixion. All
the scenes of the condemnation and death passed through his
mind and he sweated profusely. The grotesque sounds of the lash
rang and echoed around his brain, the painfully slow procession
and the writhing agony of the blood flowing freely down the

arms, the wounds opening more and more as the body heaved itself upwards in order to breathe.

"Oh, Lord spare me the agony of the cross. I don't have the courage to follow you to the cross. I am a coward and afraid I might betray you. Give me a little of your cross everyday and I can bear it, but please, please spare me. I don't have the courage."

Joseph gradually rocked himself to sleep, repeating the words over and over again "spare me, I don't have the courage." When he woke, he felt he wanted to speak to someone. He hadn't noticed his companions until then, and they had left him alone: if a man doesn't want to talk, then better to leave him to his thoughts. Some drivers walk alone and only speak at night. Others talk all the time and are a nuisance: they exhaust everybody. It is better to give everybody space. There is plenty on the march; each man to his own space, in dealing with the difficulties of the journey. Some like the noisy team effort, others the solitary way. That is the beauty of a journey, hard but free. Each to his own; company when he needs it; solitude if he cares for it. It was considered rude to ask about people's past; each man to his own privacy.

In order to spare himself another night of misery Joseph resolved never to think of his family again, to cast out the reminders as they came slipping into recesses of his mind.

# CHAPTER 8

## ⚡ Through Gaul to Britain

From then on, by an effort of will, he would think only of the present and the immediate future; the rest he would place in the hands of God.

Sanity demanded this form of renunciation. There was no profit in dwelling in the past.

The only exception he made was to recall Christ's appearance to him after his resurrection and the words he spoke to him, the look on his face as he kissed him, the hands on each side of his head, and the promise he had made to him.

This mental treasure would be currency for his hope in the future, a place to return to when loneliness would fill his heart like the cold and damp of a cave.

Northern Gaul was beautiful as they neared the coast. They kept to the high ground avoiding as far as possible the swamps and the dense forest.

Sometimes the tracks went through woodland swamps, the dense brambles and fallen rotting trees pushed to one side; and wattle and brush roadways pressed into the swamp to give a precarious solidity to the ground underneath.

Great care had to be taken with the animals to prevent them from skittering sideways into the marsh. The donkeys gave little problem, their carefully measured step negotiating the pathway, although they did try to brush against the trees in order to shed their load, and he, with a little stick for encouragement, let them know he was aware of their tricks.

The horses sometimes refused to budge, creating lots of cursing and shouting from the drivers.

To solve this, Joseph suggested a train—horses in a long line with donkeys placed at intervals along the line, their quietness and patience having a calming effect on the more excitable animals, and with the most troublesome horses blindfolded. He had seen his father use this method on difficult mountain passes where a mistake meant a death plunge to the valley below.

Joseph's apparent experience in moving goods earned him respect from the other travelers, especially from the horsemen, who were now markedly less tired and strained than on previous journeys.

Since he spoke more languages than the others and was especially fluent in Roman, his advice or help was sought, especially as his head for figures was useful in the negotiations over rent for camp and fees for passage.

His cleverness at arranging a bargain en route or gaining extra pack animals as the need arose, earned him the profound respect of the owner. He had made more money on this trip than ever before and lost fewer beasts to the marshes and his natural generosity extended his extra revenue to include Joseph.

After each transaction, a portion of the profit found its way into Joseph's possession, usually with a smile a nod and a wink, and a flourish of the hand. It became quite a ritual.

The owner, Morvah, was a pleasant man. Very strong, jovial, yet sensitive enough to leave Joseph alone when, after his gifts, Joseph quietly smiled but sought no further conversation. He realized he was a man with a great trouble and had not taken offence.

Yet he welcomed Joseph's gradual abandonment of his reserve and the return to a lighter spirit and good humor. They began to drink and converse in Roman in the evenings by the fire; Joseph asked him many questions about the country, the tribes and about what life was like in Britain. It was from him that he learned his first words of British. "Yes, No, thank you, toilet," useful words in any new language.

Morvah also owned ships, or at least his family had ships, that regularly crossed the channel between Britain and Gaul. Trade was mostly in tin and lead, with some gold in exchange for rope, cloth of all types, dyes, spices, and perfumes. British bronzes had also become popular, and these carried higher profit. It was a side of the business which he wanted to develop, but he was ignorant of the eastern Mediterranean. This made him very dependent on the merchants of Marsalla. He felt that with greater knowledge he could obtain better prices. His knowledge of Mediterranean languages was rudimentary.

He was fascinated by Joseph's quick brain, that Joseph could write signs and then repeat words of British back to him. He taught Joseph many words related to the animals, the food they ate and the plants they passed on the way. In the evening Joseph would repeat them back to him having spent the journey learning them by heart. Morvah was a patient teacher and was not happy until the pronunciation was correct using the right parts of the mouth, lips and tongue. A natural actor, prone to gesticulation and dramatic speech, Joseph advanced under his tutelage. Shouting out the new words to the trees until all the other drivers began to repeat the lesson mockingly, introducing rhyming words of a crude nature as their participation in the lesson. Joseph with Morvah's help built up a store of repartee and his quick mind brought instant hilarity when the occasion arose.

Time began to pass very quickly and Joseph's care for the others made him popular. He could cook better than the others and gradually improved the diet, sometimes adding a few spices from his backpack, according to his tradition. He even translated the blessing for the meal into British with Morvah's help; and the drivers listened in silent approval, followed by a nod of the head at the end. Morvah had held his audience with his finger pointing upwards, his eyes sharp and piercing like a true Thespian.

Moments for drama are few on the long repetitive journeys, walking with the animals; and the evening meal is always the high point of the day. Joseph had improved it and given it mystery, invoking a God of Israel, they had all heard about. The travelers knew only too well the dangers of voyage in foreign lands, how little protection they had, and therefore appreciated blessings wished for them or received.

It was one of Morvah's ships that was to take them across the channel. Morvah was surprised that Joseph wished to cross with him and he invited him to stay at his house. A mixture of Roman and British had brought about a fairly comfortable dialogue between them. Conversation became easier and easier as each day passed. Joseph kept accounts for Morvah in writing and read them back to him each evening, keeping track of expenditures and profits on each leg of the journey. Morvah had never been so organized.

"What do you want to do in Britain?" Morvah eventually asked Joseph.

"I don't know," was the reply.

"Are you escaping?"

"Yes"

"Who from?"

"Roman injustice"

"Bastards. They already cripple me with taxes as I pass through Gaul and would do so even more if I told them everything. There are some Romans in Fal, where we are going. They buy metal and sell slaves. Some say they are spies, planning for invasion, but they are helping the British against the Belgian tribes who've taken over the eastern part of the country and are driving out the British. They are giving advice on the construction of forts to stop the Belgians from moving westward."

Embarkation was from a small rotting jetty off the coast where a huge sweep of a river met the sea. It was sheltered, hot and humid with the fetid smell of rotting seaweed and fish. The horses were stabled, and the donkeys let out into a field next to the stables to await the return journey. The stores were loaded on small ships; a great deal of effort was put into securing the cargo, tying it down and covering it with rough cloth. The ship looked sturdy, though a little clumsy with large cross beams and a heavy rudder strongly attached by very thick rope.

They set out with a strong breeze blowing down the river and helped by the current made good headway out to sea. It was the first time Joseph had experienced such biting cold. The wind seemed to cut through his clothing and the gray sky showed no sign of giving way to blue; gray from horizon to horizon and a dark gray green ocean. The waves hit the ship, which yawed, rolled, and pitched, with men on the rudder heaving and cursing while trying to hold the ship on some course without any apparent landmarks to guide them. They were lost in a sea of gray, no land to be seen in the driving mist and spray. The sailors seemed to know what they were doing, and Joseph did not unduly concern himself. His apprehension of landing in a new country, and the cold, which made him crouch out of the wind, occupied body and spirit. He thanked God and Tobit and Raphael for giving him Morvah as companion. How could he have faced Britain without him?

"Too rough to eat now Boyo. You'll have a good meal when we get home, hot as a volcano, with lots of meat," came the cry from the poop.

Joseph's first view of Britain was of towering black rock and rushing water. The boat headed for an inlet leading to a stone jetty. Slats of cold white light occasionally played on the sea and rocks and then on dark cold water and forested hills, vivid green, dense impenetrable forests and rocky crags rising out of the forests, black and forbidding. The cries of the sea birds echoed everywhere as they glided behind the ship, their heads bent sideways looking down on the ship as they sped past. He could see smoke rising from the forest near the tops of the mountain, heavy black smoke; too heavy for domestic dwellings, he thought. The boat headed up river as far as it would go, and a similar jetty to the one they had left awaited them. The smell was even stronger: pungent sea weed and fish plus the strong smell of wood-smoke and animal dung. Oxen and goats seemed to wander aimlessly round the jetty idly chewing anything that could be chewed. They were fat lazy animals; they had grazing food in plenty. They did not even move out of the way as the sailors struggled up the path carrying their loads to the sheds well above sea level in a part of the hillside sheltered from the sea wind. The village rested below the brow of a hill, which separated them from the sea winds. The village looked north away from the sun and the wind. It was dark and damp with the musty smell of decaying timber and wet thatch. Mud was everywhere mixed with fresh dung, dark gray-black like the sea streaked with yellow. Dried grass and straw lay heaped and scattered round the central area of the village; a few chickens clucked in wattle cages, safe from the dogs, which roamed casually through the buildings keeping a careful eye on one another.

"Blonwen, Blonwen, where are you, my screaming passion?" Morvah shouted at the top of his Thespian voice.

"Back already? I wasn't expecting you for another week." Out came a short plump lady brushing her hair—a process that started at the first call from below. One or two little replicas were already running down the path, instantly recognizing the voice and shouting that they had heard him: a wild jump into his arms and a slow walk up the hill with two extra live burdens on his arms as well as the special packages brought from the ship.

"I've brought a gentleman from the east to stay with us until he gets settled. He is going to help me deal with the traders in Marsalla. Knows a thing or two about trade in those parts, he does."

"Well there's always a place in the barn for your friends. You know that. Come in, you must be frozen. Cold wet summer we've 'ad this year indeed."

Joseph was now wet with sweat since he had struggled up the hill. His arms ached with the two packs, and his feet were wet with mud. His rope sandals slid over his feet as he walked; the mud had got between them and the soles of his feet, and the sandals slipped in the mud: a rather ungainly approach. He sat on

a bench by the fire as the smoke drifted up to the thatch. Light came through the open door. There were no windows: the rest was gloom.

A bowl of hot broth was pushed into his hand followed by a large piece of black bread. An earthenware pot of mead was pushed to his side with a smaller earthenware cup beside it. He had tasted mead with Morvah in Gaul and was aware of its potency. The broth scalded his mouth, and he cooled it with the mead. The large lumps of fresh meat tasted good. Fresh meat was expensive in the east and reserved for the rich. Life here has some compensations, he thought.

There was an animated conversation between Morvah and his wife, interrupted by romps with the children that Joseph couldn't follow. There was an occasional gesture in his direction from Morvah followed by a smile and a look from the wife and the slow look of curiosity from the children who overcame their shyness to show him the presents brought for them by Morvah.

Eventually everyone grew tired, and Morvah indicated where Joseph was to sleep. He led him to a barn next to the house with a ladder leading up the side into the gloom. He climbed it to the top and then stepped sideways through an opening into a pile of hay, kept in a loft above the animals. A goodnight shout from Morvah, and he was left alone.

It was now quite dark and Joseph arranged the hay as well as he could and settled down to sleep.

Crack! His backside broke something as his weight settled in the hay. He knew the sound—breaking eggs. In the dark he had settled on a clutch of eggs and had broken them. His hand felt the gooey mass behind him. Should he go down and try to wash it off, or should he stay and tough it out for the night? The smell was already quite strong, and he knew he wouldn't get much sleep. He crept for the narrow hatchway and then down the ladder. Barking dogs greeted his movements around the yard to the stream. He tried to wipe off the slime as well as he could with wet grass and then more liberally as he got to the stream.

"Now is hardly the time for joking, Lord," he complained under his breath as he gingerly felt his way back to the barn in the inky blackness. He crept up the ladder, felt the hay carefully and then slowly settled down.

He wept, wet and uncomfortable in the hay, ashamed of himself for shedding tears over such a trivial event.

He slept fitfully during the night; but as dawn came he went into a deep sleep, slipping deeper into the warm hay, burying his head to keep out the light.

Everyone was up and about when he finally descended the ladder. There were gestures from the family to come and eat, but he indicated he was going to wash. He went to a private part of the stream where bushes went to the waters' edge and a flat rock covered with running water afforded a convenient place to stand just before the stream entered the rock pond. It had been dammed at one end to provide water for the rare occasions when water was scarce. The pool was quite deep.

As he went through his ablutions according to Tradition, he noticed one of the young village girls, of the type that generally hang around the docks, deliberately washing herself upstream and looking in his direction. Word was out already of the stranger in the village. Joseph slowly slipped up to his neck in the water and was really quite angry.

"Lord, that is enough. If that girl doesn't go, then I stay here until I am dead. I shall never marry a gentile, against our Law. If you don't stop this I shall complain to Mary."

"What are you doing, drowning your fleas?" A fierce voice, speaking Roman, came drifting through the trees.

"No, I sat on a clutch of eggs last night and I thought I would wash off the slime and wash myself at the same time." A woman with flaming red hair blowing in the breeze stood by the pool.

"I wouldn't stay too long in there if I was you. The water comes straight down from the mountains. You'll die of the cold."

Joseph slowly crawled gingerly out of the pool and stood there, shivering. The girl came running down to help him.

"Be off! If any of you girls bother this man . . . I'll eat her liver." The girl did not slow down, merely changed direction and was off.

"No need to send a dragon with its head on fire, oh Lord," thought Joseph.

"Do you have a change of clothes?

By the way, my name is Eleanor."

"Joseph.

"Well no, I meant to get something when I arrived here." The words came out between shivers.

"My husband was about your size. You can come and try them on. Or better I can send some here, and you can try them on," when she quickly detected a reluctance to follow. "I'll go and tell my servant to bring them."

She turned and left, and Joseph tried to dry himself, as well as he could, squeezing out the water with his hands.

The clothes arrived, some of them cloth, Roman fashion. Joseph chose a strong fabric tunic and a short leather cloak, fastened with a buckle over one shoulder. He gave in to the luxury of drying himself with one of the cloths, sent for the purpose.

"Please, tell your mistress thank you." Joseph said in British and returned to the house. An admiring applause greeted his entry.

"Ah, Eleanor," said Morvah "big woman around here, very fierce. Husband killed in battle. He chose the soft option rather than live with a woman like that." Feminine laughter trickled out from inside the house. "She came from an important tribe to the North. Marriage was a kind of treaty between their tribe and ours. Now she's a widow and head of the clan. She never had children. Very, very clever woman. Much too intelligent and independent for the men round 'ere."

# CHAPTER 9

## ⚘ A Place to Stay

During the next few weeks Joseph began to settle down. He rented a house, a modest affair, two rooms, but with the possibility of a small garden. It had a thatched roof in fairly good condition, and a stream trickled out of the rocks where the garden ended against a small cliff face. The front of the house faced the sea but a slight mound prevented a sea view. The front land could also be developed as it extended towards the sea. The house had no windows, but there were two holes covered by boards, in addition to the door, to give extra ventilation during the rare hot summer days. A flat stone in the middle of one room had the charred remains of a fire. The smoke was allowed to drift out through the gaps in the thatch. Stone seating was arranged around the fire, and the stones also served as low tables for cooking. Stone ledges were arranged for the storage of the cooking pot and earthenware utensils. The metal cooking pot had disappeared with the previous owner, being more valuable than the house itself. The bed was a straw mat with hay thrown on top, serving as blanket. This lay in a slight recess in the mud and wattle wall in the second room. A door separated the two rooms and wooden hooks incorporated into the door structure lay behind both doors.

Purchase of goods was largely by barter and as Joseph, as yet, had nothing with which to barter, Morvah supplied him with essential commodities. His wife sent over hot meals in a pot by one of the children, which Joseph carefully washed and returned promptly.

Joseph used one of the stone ledges to do the accounts, though it was difficult because of lack of light, especially on bleak rainy days. Writing was with a slab of white clay and a die extracted from a fungus. Care had to be taken with the brush, keeping it fairly dry to prevent the ink spreading into a messy blob. Turning a page meant wiping off the old clay and spreading fresh clay from a damp pot in the corner. Temporary accounts were done in this fashion. More permanent ones could be done on velum, expensive, or with brown clay, using a sharp stick to mark grooves, then carefully wetting the grooves and blowing chalk onto the plate of clay. This could then be baked. The grooves could be painted to make them more legible afterwards.

The Sumerians had used a similar technique. There was no Egyptian paper. Joseph longed for decent paper, but he kept his patience and gradually developed the art of the new writing. He took pride and care in his work. The results were read out to Morvah, followed by planning talks on what to do next. Morvah's pleasant manner and openness gave him many contacts. He ran many enterprises, timber, boat building, ship outfitting and the making of iron and bronze castings for tackle for ships, horses, carts, and chariots. The chariots were Eastern in design. Morvah had kept all these business transactions in his head. He had a prodigious memory, but was grateful for extra help and counsel.

Morvah gave Joseph part of the business, dealing with trade at Marsalla. He had tired of the long journeys and wanted to spend more time at home here in Fal with his wife and children. He knew Joseph would do this part of the work more competently and he would bring good business for his ships.

# CHAPTER 10

## ❧ A Visit to the Chief

Having acquired a new set of clothes, Joseph carefully cleaned the borrowed clothing, folded it and set off to return it. He struggled hard to think of a gift. He wrote out a poem by Horace from memory with a suitable quote referring to the icy stream.

He etched out the words in clay, baked it carefully along with a few cartoon drawings to decorate the edges. He then colored grooves carefully with a collection of inks and dyes of different colors. Holes had been pierced in the clay to allow fixing before baking.

At the sixth attempt, he got one up to satisfactory standard. He made a smooth wooden box that fitted the plate and set out for the house.

The Chief's house stood on a hill surrounded by a palisade. A narrow path led diagonally up the hill to the gate. A wide field lay inside the gate with houses at one corner. They were of more careful construction than in the village below. The beams had been pinioned carefully and the spaces in between the beams filled with wattle and mud mixed with cow-dung and animal blood. The outside had been carefully smoothed and window frames had been constructed, covered with waxed velum. A garden with shrubs and flowers lay outside the chief's hut, much better than ever he could have mustered. Bringing flowers had never seemed appropriate. It was also too closely associated with pagan rituals and he could never be sure of the symbolism behind bringing flowers.

A maidservant answered the knock and showed him into the hut. The room contained wooden benches and a table with one placed under the parchment window. The window was south facing and the light falling on the table was quite good. The window was large and had outer shutters.

"Good morning," Eleanor came into the room. She showed evidence of hasty grooming, since she had seen him enter the stockade.

"We are not often graced by foreign visitors. Her Roman came out slowly and thoughtfully, still evidently translating from British as she spoke. A maidservant brought out mead and honey cakes, placed them on the table between them and left.

"I would like to thank you for the loan of the clothes at such a difficult time. Your help was a gift from heaven." Joseph spoke sincerely. "I have copied an extract from a poem by a famous Roman poet, Horace. May I read it out to you?" Eleanor smiled and nodded.

Joseph read slowly hoping she would follow the Latin.

Musis amicua tristitiam et metus
tradam protervis in mare Creticum
portare ventis quis sub Arcto
rex gelidae metuatur orae

Dear to the Muses I will banish
gloom and fear to the wild winds
to carry o'er the Cretan Sea,
all unconcerned what rulers
of the frozen borders of the North
is object of our fear, or what danger
—*Carminum Liber I*

She smiled at the frozen borders of the North.

"May I ask you a question. Why have you come here? You are obviously well educated. Why here?"

"To escape the Romans. They killed my entire family and confiscated my property."

"How terrible! My husband was killed, and now I too am a stranger in a foreign land. I am a Chun, not a Dumnon." Eleanor paused for dramatic effect.

"Oh I hadn't realized." Joseph pretended that he knew the significance.

"Oh yes, I am not from these parts. When news of my husband's death came to me I thought of killing myself as well. . . . When they brought his mangled body to me. . . . There is no describing the grief."

"I was spared that part. I escaped before I could be sold into slavery and I last saw them as I left for Jerusalem. A normal family."

"Loneliness is one of the hardest of griefs to bear. Tell me: why did you react like that at the watering pool?"

"I told you, I needed to clean off some egg yolk."

"Liar. I saw a man before, washing like that. You are from Israel. This Jew I am talking about was killed in an argument over payment, and I have his books which were among his belongings."

She went into the other room and came back with a large beautifully carved box. She opened it, and it contained scrolls of the Law and the Prophets.

Joseph said a prayer for the dead soul as he looked through them. "These are finely written."

"On some days I open this box and run my fingers over the writing; the writing looks so magical . . .

"If you can teach me how to read these skins, I will pay."

"If you get ten, no, twelve people, who will study with you, I will teach you to write Roman to communicate with the Romans, and Hebrew and Aramaic to communicate with God."

"I already write Roman" came the fierce reply, angry that he should think her illiterate.

Joseph started, like a gladiator who realized he had made a false move in front of the beast and risked getting devoured.

"Oh no, I meant some of the Roman poets. Do you think you can get twelve?"

"Of course. Do you think we are all unintelligent round here? Just off the farm?"

Joseph mentally sank to his knees before the gaping jaws, bade his farewell, then fled. A gladiator trick, when things are not going well. Appear to leave casually, when it is in real fact: escape.

"By tomorrow," a defiant call as he left. "Come early in the morning."

CHAPTER 11

## ⚜ First Lessons

E arly morning and twenty people were assembled: women friends and a few boys and girls chosen for their cleverness. She had obviously been teaching them to write in Roman.

Joseph started in the beginning in both senses, the Hebrew letters, and to give light relief to the lesson, he told them the stories, starting with the beginning of everything.

He tried his best at drama; to an audience used to story telling, it lacked the subtlety of the British, and he therefore decided to concentrate on getting over the meaning of the Prophets.

It was this that drew their attention. Statements, that he had grown up with and had taken for granted had startling effect. Here were new minds, innocent, uncluttered with the mental corruptions of an over-sophisticated society.

He hurried home in the mid afternoon, exhausted by the grueling timetable, sleepy from the huge meal provided by the host, and minus a cloak held back for repair. He thought about how to reconcile his two jobs. Early morning, first light, accounts, then lesson preparation, then off to lessons. Dusk, prayer—prayer for success.

God had given him opportunity. "You must do the writing and the speaking, Lord. I am not able. I am not able."

Joseph was excited, yet apprehensive. He was alone, faced with the task of explaining the religion of the God of Israel. What could he say of the Messiah? He only met Him once after the Resurrection. Yet His instructions were clear.

Days passed, weeks passed, Joseph looked healthier and more cheerful. His day was fully occupied. The early morning dawn and the plan for the day were back in his schedule.

Early to sleep, when light was no longer available, plus endless odd moments redesigning the house, giving it some of the amenities of his house in Jerusalem. Velum windows to bring in more light. Flat stones for the floor—with iron tools he began to cut the stone and shape it. He wanted a shelter over the brow and looking out to sea. It would be of stone, strong enough to withstand the wind. He baked tiles for the roof and designed the timbers. He would use charcoal for the fire with small vents to the outside of the house to prevent suffocation. A dry stone wall sheltered the dwelling from the wind except from the immediate south. The spaces between the stones were filled with chopped moss, chalk and clay, as they were laid, to keep out the wind. He did not have the time to grind the stones flat. Rubble and flat stones formed a patio for work outside when weather permitted.

His first year was consolidation. From his classes, he also improved his British, and a great deal of his mental effort went into his classes.

He found the winter bearable. He had experienced snow in the Taurus Mountains. Here in this part of Britain there had been no snow, at least on the low lands near the sea.

Days passed quickly, as his ability to make conversation grew. Eleanor was the female equivalent of Morvah, though not so easygoing. She had a quick eye for detail and was not satisfied until everything was just right. She was very demanding, as a pupil, and ruled everyone . . . including Joseph.

Three years passed.

# CHAPTER 12

# ❧ A Roman Encounter

The summer sailing season had been underway for some weeks, and Joseph decided to walk down the jetty by the river. It was a beautiful hot summer day. He now had had experience of four British summers. His classes had grown.

Through contacts in Gaul he had managed to obtain scripts of classical learning. His pupils had transcribed some of the Holy Writings onto velum. They were learning the scriptures by heart. He had gone to the jetty to see if any more books had been brought in on a ship that had just docked. A group of Romans, just disembarked, were by the jetty.

"Oh what have we here! One of the local creatures" the accent was affected Pompeii, but it was phoney.

Joseph pretended not to notice.

"I find if you talk very slowly and a little louder, the locals always understand.

"Hello, oh ye great unwashed" and the Roman held Joseph's beard. The Roman was too ignorant to realize he was outside Roman jurisdiction and actions like that could get him killed.

"Take me to your leader." The joke fell flat.

Joseph's anger mounted. The superficial arrogance, the thick mind of a soldier, the pretension to learning and memories of his last encounter with a similar Roman boiled and fumed inside his breast—hatred and bitter memory rushing from the dark corners of his mind in underground torrents. A dagger thrust—then what would he do with the other Romans? He would have no chance against them all.

He could arrange to have them all killed later. What would Eleanor's reaction be like? And the children? The various possibilities presented themselves to his mind.

Eventually, after a few more biting comments at his expense and seeing that he was getting nowhere the Roman took away his hand.

With the loud comment "This place needs a bit of Roman civilization" he returned to his companions. He had been daring in front of his companions, but not too daring; after all, his companions were near, and they would have pulled around if he had got into trouble.

A crack of the whip brought the slaves off the ship.

Joseph returned home slowly. Since he had wanted not to reveal he spoke Latin, the reason for his visit had been curtailed. He would contact the ship later.

Joseph's anger did not subside, nor could he think straight, when he got back home. Fury would make him stand up and walk around the room. his inadequacy and cowardice when faced with the Roman: his chance of vengeance had slipped by—in cowardice. Reason had been the cloak to hide his lack of courage.

"Oh Lord, you have a coward on your hands."

"An eye for an eye and a tooth for a tooth. Is this your Jewish justice?" The thoughts slipped through his mind like a snake, insidiously, like the snake in the Garden of Eden.

"The man only humiliated you. Is this proportionate?" the thoughts lingered. "Proportionate. Proportionate." Joseph knew the law.

"Proportionate."

Were a few words of ridicule from a bone-thick ignoramus reason for a death sentence? And the Roman bystanders, were they to die too?

Seven hundred and fifty men, the entire cohort in Jerusalem, in full array, to say: "Hail, King of the Jews." An entire cohort: And Jesus, God of Creation, allowed it. The thoughts and the memories flowed through Joseph's mind.

The Redeemer, promised to Israel, had allowed it.

Joseph made a small cross out of some pieces of wood there, and he kissed it. He held it to his breast, and then he wept.

# CHAPTER 13

## ⚶ The Making of Bronze

Next morning Joseph hurried up the hill to class carrying his newly made cross. His lessons in writing were distracted.

The scripture lesson began with Moses in the desert, how the people were being bitten by snakes and they began to complain. And Moses made a bronze serpent on a pole, and anyone who had been bitten and looked onto the bronze snake was cured of his affliction.

"Now can any of you explain this passage to me?"

"Snakes won't bite you if you keep away from them. Snakes won't chase you. It would have been much easier if they had kept out of the way."

"In Britain we sometimes use the word snake to mean people who are vindictive. They always want to snap back at someone and get revenge for any wrong done to them." The words of a girl came floating down from the back of the room.

"Exactly. The snake could be a general word for a state of mind of the Jewish people; they were beset by quarrels and dissension . . .

"Contemplation of the snake could mean that, in this way, they could overcome their hatred for each other, overcome their quarrels and live with each other in peace. It is very difficult sometimes to know if the scriptures are referring to real events or are allegorical.

"The bronze serpent of Moses prefigured the Cross of Jesus. He came to save the world from the destructiveness of hate. This is what Genesis means, when God promised that a woman would crush the head of the serpent Satan. The fruit of her womb would be the promised Messiah, who would heal the wounds left by sin . . . by his own wounds. The wounds of sin would be cured by the wounds of love. The head of the snake would be replaced by the face of Jesus. This is how I interpret the meaning of this passage."

Then Joseph recounted in vivid detail his experience of meeting Jesus, and the events leading to the crucifixion. The tears streaked his beard as he described each event. It was late evening when he finally ended with his description of Jesus' appearance to him after the Resurrection; how he held his head.

He struggled to remember the strange phrasing.

He had said: "I am the full knowledge that the Father has of himself; Father and I are one, and the love of us will proceed from us and it will embrace you with a love greater than the love of all the mothers in the world. Be faithful to me, Joseph, and I will come and abide with you physically, in person, before you leave this world."

"That was the promise Jesus made to me in person. This means that some day Jesus will come, if I am to stay here, and walk on this land of Britain . . .

"Let us prepare for His coming. Let us work with utmost diligence that there will be many people to greet Him when he comes. He will bring a message to us. Let us have many people who will have understanding of the Law and the Prophets when he comes. Amen."

Eleanor took him by the arm and led him to the stockade gate. It was dark and the others followed. "Goodnight, Joseph! You have given us more than enough to think about for one night."

Eleanor was happy, very happy. Her suspicions about Joseph had been dispelled that evening. She had seen the man, underneath the politeness and reserve.

She had also known isolation. She remembered how she had prayed to the God of the Jews, to come and help her in her loneliness and utter emptiness. This God had actually replied to her, via Joseph.

"Imagine—God's sending him all this way—just for me."

# CHAPTER 14

# ⚘ The Chief Bard

Later in the week Eleanor called Joseph to her house. "I have been thinking Joseph. People here like symbols, reminders of their deities, of their spirits. A snake is already one of our symbols. It too symbolizes evil, poison. We can cast snakes in bronze just as the Jews. Would you like a bronze serpent to help in your teaching? I can have one made for you."

Joseph thought for a moment,

"I would like a serpent which bears the face of Christ instead of the serpent's head. This is the new serpent we preach. The face of Christ crucified who died for our sins.

"Give me a few days and I will try to do the impossible and draw the face of Christ for your craftsmen."

It was a few months before the bronze actually arrived from the casting. Joseph went to collect it from the foundry.

It was about a quarter of the size of a man, a bronze snake around the stem of a cross with the head of Christ looking out in the expression he remembered, as he spoke the words of the Psalm.

Joseph was disappointed with the face. But how could it be possible for bronze to capture such a moment?

"If you had seen a real crucifixion, you would not be carrying something like that." The words came from one of the slave traders, taking a group of replacement slaves to the mine.

"I have seen the deaths of crucified slaves, who have killed Romans, in trying to escape. . . . Such occasions are very rare, thank the heavens, but on those occasions the Romans nail their victim through the wrist and ankle to the cross. And to breathe the victim has to raise himself, bearing his full weight on the nails. The one I saw screamed himself to death! "The screams of these slaves going down the mine is nothing compared with a real Roman execution of a slave."

"Why do the slaves scream so much when they are lowered down the mine?" asked Joseph.

"The slaves are given a rudimentary training in digging tunnels, how to recognize good ore and how to load it in baskets for lifting out, up the shaft on the hoist. They are then lowered one by one hooked by their shackles to the rope of the hoist and then lowered down the mine to the waiting guards below.

"They scream because that is the last time they see daylight. These slaves enter Hades early. Once they go down there, not even death brings them out of the mine. They leave the bodies in one part of the mine for the rats to eat. Even the guards do not go down the tunnels, they stay near the mine entrance. They have to be tough and good fighters. They barter food for ore with the slaves. The strongest slaves are the team leaders; they are the ones who deal directly with the guards. They eat their fill to keep themselves strong and pass on the food remains to the next strongest in the pack in exchange for ore and so on. The weak and the sick only get the droppings and the cast off food. There are no old people down in the mines. Average life is five years. The worst death is the sick team leader's. Once his strength has gone the others vent their rage on him, torturing him to death as slowly as they can. Only the fittest survive and then not for long."

Joseph sat for a while looking at the new casting and the face resting on the cross. He then slowly went over to the mine owner.

"My friend, I have a proposition for you."

"What is it?"

"It is not good for man to work without hope. I would like to suggest to you a new way."

"Are you referring to the mine?"

"Yes. I would like to make a proposition. Give these men the Sabbath rest according to my religion, bringing them out of the mine for one day a week, so that they may know about my God and I will pay for any loss of production if any occurs. I do not want you to give an answer now, but in a few days time."

For the next few days Joseph fasted, praying for hours in front of the cross in his room. He prayed like his ancestors of old in the desert waiting to be cured of the poison sting, the venom of hatred that bathed their heart.

As he hungered he thought of the slaves dying in the bowels of the earth, and he was moved.

On the eve of the Sabbath Joseph climbed the hill to the mine for his appointment with the owner. A small crowd of curious onlookers followed, including his pupils and teachers, who he had asked to join him in prayer and fasting. The owner was slightly unnerved by the stares of these onlookers and the anxious looks on their faces.

"Do you agree my friend? I will take full responsibility for the consequences and recompense you in full if any loss occurs."

A little girl ran forward spontaneously, held the mine owner's hand and put her head on his arm to await the outcome. The emotional tyranny of the little girl proved too great, and he relented to a huge cheer from the crowd.

Joseph, his heart pounding like foundry hammers, was lowered down the mine shaft. The guards took him to the slave leaders for a conference. Joseph explained the proposition and the need to maintain production even though they would be working only six days. There was no difficulty in securing their agreement. One by one they were chained to prevent escape and hoisted up the shaft. When the last had been hoisted Joseph took a lamp and began to walk the tunnels of the cave. All the guards left by a staircase cut in the rock, the first part being a ladder lowered from above to prevent escape. One guard remained. Nazim chose to remain. In the last revolt of the slaves he had been the one who had defeated them. Singled-handed he had killed the slave leaders as they attacked him with picks and axes when the other guards had fled before the onslaught. He remembered his fear and cold deep depression after the event. And now he was fascinated by this man going unarmed into the tunnels.

The first specimens of humanity shocked Nazim. Men simply had died and rotted away in the darkness, and he never saw them. Only the strongest gained the most advantageous positions of being near the guards. He called for baskets and placed the living heaps of bones and skin onto them for hoisting up into the air. The guard blindfolded them to protect them from the pain of daylight.

The next group revolted him. Flesh half eaten by rats, gnawed bare to the bone—living skeletons too weak to fend off their adversaries, gliding about in the darkness. He rolled them in coarse cloth and lifted them into the basket, unable to touch them.

Joseph returned time and time again into the darkness, a bobbing light casting large shadows onto the wall, which seemed to fall rapidly to the floor of the tunnel as his light passed down each branch of the labyrinth and down the ladders into the lower galleries.

Finally came the remains of the bodies for burial each carefully wrapped in cloth provided by the guard and bound with rope.

When Joseph finally emerged empty handed to the base of the shaft his clothes reeked with the sickly putrid odor of death and decay. His face was frozen, drawn with fatigue, shock and fear.

Nazim the guard helped him up the ladder. He too felt sick, but his occupation had accustomed him to horror. Joseph looked at Nazim kindly. "I will have need of you in the future, Nazim," he said to him in poor Phoenician.

On the surface, some of the women were already rushing about with vinegar and oil to clean the wounds. Their shrieks and cries brought other women out of the village, and they too joined in tending to the sick.

The men sat and watched with curiosity as each new body came out. Some were eventually co-opted by the womenfolk into carrying ready-made stretchers of wooden planks, tearing up cloth for bandages, and lighting fires to prepare soft foods for the sick. Some of those brought up died, the excitement proving too much in their weakened condition.

When Joseph emerged there was total silence as he walked slowly to the cross at the top of the mine, knelt before it for a few moments, and then kissed it. Eleanor handed him a wet towel to wash his hands and face, and then offered him a bowl of soup. He accepted the towel but declined the soup.

When the slaves had been fed and washed, and had rested a little, he led them in a prayer of thanksgiving to the Almighty God who had delivered them temporarily out of bondage.

"Slaves, I too know what it is to suffer the cruel yoke of slavery. My period of slavery was extremely short. I was fortunate indeed. Why does God allow such suffering?

"I cannot give you an answer. But I have seen God face to face. God became man, lived, and suffered, far more than your suffering, suffered humiliation far greater than your humiliation, and met an ignominious death nailed to a cross.

"He did this willingly . . . for our sins, for your sins and my sins, and to show us a way to conquer fear and suffering. The mystery of suffering is indeed a mystery, it is beyond our reason. . . . We must accept it because Christ accepted it and therefore our acceptance of it must be important to him in some way . . .

"Only faith in the goodness of God sustains us. . . . I hope you will suffer your hardships for love of God. I hope you will bear with each other deep in the darkness of the Earth. I hope you will love one another as he has loved us . . .

"God has promised a heavenly reward for those who love him. As he said himself 'Eye has not seen or ear heard the things that I have prepared for those who love me.'

"I hope you will turn your slavery, your hovel down below, into a treasure house of love, because out of that treasure house

will come all good things of the spirit. Bear your sufferings for
love of God. For in some mysterious way the betterment of the
world depends on your sacrifice. A light came into the world
with the birth of Jesus Christ which cannot be extinguished.
Remember that light in your soul as you work down there, just as
you will look forward to daylight in the midst of your toils. Jesus
descended into a tomb only to emerge at the resurrection. You too
will descend soon into the earth again, to emerge soon at each
new Sabbath in anticipation of the glorious resurrection, when we
shall meet God face to face for eternity."

As the men rested, Eleanor came rushing to Joseph. "The
women are very worried: the owner wants the sick and dying
down the mine at the end of the day. He says that otherwise the
slaves will mutilate themselves to escape from working."

Joseph tried reasoning. They sat at table while Eleanor
brought dainty dishes to place at the owner's elbow. All to no
avail; Ogof remained obdurate.

"Oh Ogof, I remember how kind your family was to me when
I came here," said Eleanor, her eyes filled with tears and her voice
tinged with desperation. "Surely these sick are no threat to you.
Let their remaining days be in peace and light . . . not dying in
despair alone and in darkness." Ogof shook his head.

Suddenly a hog's head was slammed on the table in front of
them. Flies disturbed by the movement soon settled back on the
eyes and the mouth.

Mulfra was a well-known bard in the area, well-known and
feared. Though his blue clothes represented peace, people feared
him because of the curses he could conjure on those that would
not obey him. The priests of Britain were of three kinds: white
robed Druids, who represented truth and holiness: blue robed
Bards, who promoted peace; and green robed Ovates, who studied medicine and astronomy. Mulfra was the chief Bard.

Mulfra looked at Ogof, spat, and pulled out his own tongue
so far that it rested on the bottom of his chin.

His fierce look turned Ogof's blood to water. He had heard
of the curses of Mulfra and their consequences.

"All right. But one mutilation and it's all off." Ogof quickly left the scene incapable of controlling subsequent events while Mulfra was around.

Mulfra looked at Joseph and Joseph noted a slight glint of humor deep in his fierce red eyes. The look was almost as if to say; you may be daring, but you know little about controlling men and manipulating their fears. It was the look a professional might give to an amateur.

"At your winter solstice, I want you to use the holly and the mistletoe as symbols of Christ's wounds, the holly berry for the blood of Christ and the mistletoe for the face of Christ—the face that loved us unto death. I know these plants have deep significance for you in your religion, but I am asking you to give these symbols to Christ. He is never anyone's debtor, and he will reward you richly in spirit." The words left Joseph suddenly as though he was not in control of what he was saying.

Mulfra looked at Joseph who was exhausted, out of his depth, in a foreign land; knowing little of the country and its customs, its history, its folklore, and the way people thought and felt about the things around them. He barely knew the language, and he had never experienced growing up in a British village. "Oh Joseph, you are like a flea on the back of a dog, trying to whinny like a horse," Mulfra thought to himself.

"I shall give answer in a few days' time when I have consulted the Priestly Council."

During the Sabbath, Joseph rested the men as well as he could, and the women fed them. He did not burden them with pious talk. His introduction was enough. He would say more when they got stronger.

At the end of the day, Joseph lifted his finger and indicated with his eyes that it was time for the men to go down into the mine. They all walked in docile silence down the stairs used by the guards, and then the guards followed them.

During the week another sick miner came up in a basket out of the mine shaft. He had been found hidden in a recess in the mine, too frightened or too weak to answer the call of Joseph.

A new spirit was working below ground.

An answer duly came from Mulfra.

"The Council declare . . .

"We have heard of your stories and accounts of the God of Israel. Your God is a good spirit, and we welcome it. It is not for us to oppose good spirits. Neither does it behoove us to be jealous of your success with the people, for such jealousy would tempt God to anger. We will not oppose you, and if you will give us knowledge of your God we will help you in bringing the voice of Christ to this land.

"Our Druids are dedicated to the pursuit of truth and the gods, or as you say, the One God has chosen many ways to reveal his messages to us, through nature, through the things we see, hear, and touch and sometimes through people, bearers of great wisdom. We must listen to these people with care and attention because they often mean great advances in our knowledge of things. Your message affects us all. You bring truth of great importance; you bring peace. And you tell us that a great event will happen in the future, that God will walk on this land as a person like us . . .

"Druids, Bards, and Ovates will help you in your work."

From then on Joseph's work was doubled. He no longer taught his students directly but instructed the teachers, who in turn taught the new students.

He instructed the Druids directly. Many were old, too old to learn Hebrew and the sacred texts, but translations had been made by his pupils into British, using Roman script, and he used those. The British had prodigious memories and could virtually repeat a story word for word with just one hearing. Joseph taught by stories and explained their meaning carefully. And the British were born story-tellers. His teachers went out into the villages teaching the Bible stories.

It was the Bards, who suggested the "Testament Theatre," dramatic presentations of the Teachings.

Streams were dammed for the crossing of the Red Sea, and then the water released onto the chariots of the Pharaoh. The plays drew large audiences from surrounding villages. Joseph worked tirelessly in these developments, trying to make sure that no pagan thinking crept into the teaching, instructing and re-instructing his village teachers.

What surprised him most was the devotion, which the British developed for the Archangel Michael. He was the local hero.

The British had a very strong sense of good spirits and bad spirits, and the idea that good spirits defeated bad spirits and drove them all into hell appealed to their military justice.

A huge presentation had been organized by Mulfra, a born organizer and inspirer of men. He loved things on a gigantic scale; the small-minded irritated him. Every village was asked to supply chariots, uniforms and men. The devil and his men were to be dressed in red and the good spirits to be dressed in blue, the Royal Color of the British, symbol of their race, symbol of peace. Villages were chosen by lot, as to whether they would be goodies or baddies.

The person of Michael was chosen by competition, as was that of Lucifer. Competence in bow, sword, spear, horse and chariot were the deciding factors. The selection, by elimination, lasted months. Joseph had to stress that killing an opponent meant automatic de-selection from the play. He sweated with anxiety at the enthusiasm of the elimination contest. Wooden swords can still make horrible bruises, but the British took it all as part of the fun.

At last, in September when all the harvest had been gathered in, the war of the heavens began with massive fanfare of horns and drums. Villagers sought for vantage points on the hills to watch the gigantic battle take place. Captured warriors were bound, as death was not possible for Angels. Slowly the reds began to dominate the valley and hillside as group after group of the good Angels were ambushed and captured. The wave of red began to surround the hill where Michael stood in his chariot surrounded by his Archangels, and Lucifer on the opposite hillside blew bugle notes to direct his troops. At last only a few remained as one by one Michael's archangels were dragged down the slope to capture. The crowds gasped in apprehension. This was not what they had expected.

Suddenly Michael drew out a mighty bronze horn and blew it mightily. The sound echoed down the valley and out of the woods came a new army sweeping around the back of the red and releasing the captured to join their ranks. Mulfra had secretly co-opted villages from afar, unknown to the bystanders. The cheers were ecstatic.

All that remained was the final combat between Michael and Lucifer. The crowd held its breath as the chariots swept down the opposing hills towards one another. The clash of bronze and steel, wheels cleverly avoiding one another in the battle for position, each trying to maneuver to be on the sword-striking side of the opponent, catching him wrong-handed. Hand combat followed the chariot in carefully choreographed fighting, the fight ending in a somersault over the opponent and a dagger across his neck and into capture. The crowds went wild.

Then smoke began to arise from one of the woodland valleys, as the entire troop of the enemy were driven headlong and yelling into the smoke and fire of hell. The eyes of the children were wide with fear as they looked down on the smoke and fire issuing from the woods—the yells and whinnying of horses adding to the din.

People talked about the event for weeks afterwards; and children's games were always about the battle of "Michael's Mount."

Work at the mines also improved. Ogof increased his profits. It was subsequently easier to persuade him to allow the miners to earn their freedom after five years by more efficient mining and production. Joseph gave him calculations and facts and figures to persuade him about the new system.

The guards were eventually removed from the mine to be employed protecting cargo at the docks. Import and export trade had increased mightily. Even Ogof, once, ventured down into the mine, much to the appreciation of the workers.

# CHAPTER 15

## ⚜ The Minoths

The harvest had been gathered, a very good one. Early rains in the spring, a warm summer with occasional showers, and a hot autumn had made the grain crops plentiful. Everybody was happy and contented with the prospect of a trouble-free winter. Fewer animals had been slaughtered and salted because of the prospect of sufficient fodder for the winter. There was even the possibility of fresh meat during the winter, much better than the usual salt diet. Spices were far too expensive for most folks to afford, and so there was little variety in the diet during the winter months. The fear of famine was on no one's mind that autumn.

Eleanor had judged it well. The time had come for her to use her new Mediterranean teacher to achieve what had not been achieved for as long as people could remember. Namely, to establish peace between the Chuns and the Minoths.

The feud had lasted for so long that nobody could remember the cause of the dispute; but the latest topic of conversation was always the latest insult and outrage perpetrated by the other party.

Trade between the two parties was non-existent and to journey through the opposing territory was to court disaster; only the young and the brave would attempt such a venture. Thus trade between the Chuns and the coast along the valleys through the mountains westward, and conversely through the Middle Kingdom to the East, meant long and difficult detours. The Minoths controlled the gold, and the Chuns had access to the fertile grain fields of the Middle Kingdom. Each needed the other, but neither would relent.

News of Joseph's action at the mine had reached the ears of both chieftains. The wandering bards had added the story to their list, and since this was a new story it had aroused considerable interest. The bards told the story with drama and it aroused huge emotions of compassion in the simple folk. The dreaded fear of slavery lurked in the dark recesses of everybody's mind. Joseph had become a little light of hope that everyone now cherished in his breast.

The crops of the previous year for the Minoths had been disastrous; it had been a very wet summer in the west, and blight had destroyed the crops. The tribe faced starvation, and in their weakened state feared invasion by hostile tribes. The territory of the Chuns was drier and had harvested a reasonable crop.

Following Eleanor's instructions Dauwid, her father, had sent food to the Minoths during the winter and thus had saved them.

In the spring Eleanor sent messengers, both Chun and Minoth, to the opposite camps inviting them to her territory. The reply from the Minoths was guarded, but gave sufficient hope for her to offer to visit the chiefs in person. The offer was accepted.

She went first to the Minoths. This involved a perilous journey first through forest, swamp, and mountain to the north; then by boat around the bays of the coast, dancing with the treacherous tides and rip currents; landing on a coast of sand dunes; and then through the valley running east-west. Her royal robes survived the journey, and she entered the Minoth community with sufficient pomp and dignity to impress them. Even her maids were well attired.

An impressive feast was held in her honor, everyone watched her every move, judgments changing by the second. She took great care to show kindness to the wives, knowing that their impressions would be the more lasting. To the men-folk, with their lap dog eyes, she joked and flattered, bringing grunts of contentment.

Evening came, and by the flickering fire she began her soliloquy. She described in emotional detail the event at the mine: the despair alleviated, the terrible sores, the half eaten flesh, the darkness. She took them to the very bottomless pit of Hades and then brought them slowly to the surface, gradually increasing the light in their minds until they could see the sun.

She described the dying words of a miner, his bowels half eaten and hanging from his washed body. "'I prayed to the God of Israel that I could die in the light, and he answered me. He answered me.'

"I kissed him and whispered in his ear. 'He has also given light to your soul, which shall never be extinguished for all eternity. Go in peace. And when you live in that heavenly light, throw some down to us that we, who work for the moment here below, may also have hope of light eternal.'"

Men and women were weeping by the time she finished in the early hours of the morning. It was resolved then and there to do similar things in their own mines, once Joseph had visited them. By a unanimous shout, they all resolved to visit her kingdom and to hold council with the Chuns.

Eleanor left the next day, eager not to outstay her welcome, and with that dramatic eye, wanting to leave on a tide of emotion and expectancy which would carry her safely down the valley eastwards to her kinsfolk in Chun territory. She left bearing generous gifts of gold and fine skins to add to her wardrobe. Her special and warm farewell to the Chief left a lasting impression.

She held her hand behind the chief's neck as she addressed him.

"Oh Minas, I have longed to get this close to you. Hatred is a terrible thing. It is like mildew in the grain. From the outside the grain looks normal, but when grasped it falls to dust. The outer semblance being all that remains. We must carefully pick out hatred, like blight from the grain, so that the next planting shall bring forth plenty. Hatred destroys us all and produces, like the blight, bread which is bitter and poisonous."

# CHAPTER 16

## ❧ The Chun

Her stay with her brothers, sisters and kinsfolk was a joyous one. She had not visited them since the wedding with her husband, fearing the journey as it passed near the territory of the Minoths, and also fearing for her position in the tribe of her now-departed husband. Relatives of his resented her position and inheritance. The fact that she had no children saved her: the relatives were prepared to wait, and no one relished the coming conflict of rival claims by relatives for her property. So far she had kept a delicate balance of alliances, which prevented a concerted attack on her own possessions.

Her father was still alive, with the same lively humor. He still was able to manage her strong will with gentle irony and teasing ridicule. In intellectual powers he was still her master, coupled with the wisdom of years and the responsibility for the governance of the tribe: not an easy task with a rich agricultural kingdom and envious neighbors. Everyone, enemies included, considered him a good king. His judgments were quoted in neighboring kingdoms for their fairness and honesty. It was an easy task despite his age to persuade him to visit her kingdom and settle the dispute.

So it came to pass, the Minoths passed through Chun territory on their way to the Fal region, and were given mead and
sweet cake for their journey by the maidens of the Chun as they
journeyed through the land.

Eleanor had left the Chun territory ahead of them by fast
chariot with just a few horsemen in order to prepare for the visit.

The Chuns left two days after the Minoths following the
same route. Scouts ahead made sure the road was clear and free
from ambush.

Joseph and Mulfra had not been idle during Eleanor's
absence. Mulfra was familiar with alliances, having been called to
preside over earlier covenants between tribes or families.

Joseph explained to him the covenants of God with the
people of Israel and Mulfra listened with docility.

"This can only be by grace," thought Joseph, as he watched
the simple changes of expression on Mulfra's face during the
explanation.

"A mighty thing!" was Mulfra's only comment. He felt that to
say any more would weaken the strength of his words.

Eleanor's steward had organized the Feast.

And so it was that the Minoths and the Chuns were camped
on opposite hillsides of a valley close to the well of Mulfra, conve-
niently situated at one end of the valley where a raised mound of
earth was already in place, built generations previously so that
spectators in the valley could witness the ceremonies and oath-
swearing that frequently took place there. At the other end of the
valley, surrounded by gentle woodland to give shade or shelter, the
slopes flattened into an open field where the animal roasting took
place and where the cooked food could be laid out on rough tables.

The ceremony began with a mighty blast of horns. Following
the directions of the ceremonial courtiers appointed by Mulfra,
the two Kings slowly descended the hillside to the center and
walked together to their places of honor. The two hillsides slid
together in a mass of bodies as the two hillsides joined into one
on the valley floor. All faces turned to the end of the valley.

"Do you renounce enmity forever?" boomed out Mulfra, his voice magnified by a thin board and two tightly stretched parchments attached to each side like wings, which were placed just behind his head. His voice echoing down the valley was pushed back by a mighty roar of "We do!"

Before the echo had died down, the voice began again. "Do you remove all hatred of each other from your hearts?"

"We do!" came back the thunder.

"Do you renounce all insult and violations against one another?"

"We do!" came back like a wave.

Now came the interesting part of he ceremony, which once more showed the genius of Mulfra. Abstract ideas do not carry much weight with simple folk. Mulfra spelt out the detail.

"Will you avoid pissing upstream of their villages, fouling their wells and giving visible insult?"

"We will!" a slightly weaker reply came back as each remembered some insult either directly experienced or vividly recounted.

Slowly Mulfra spelt out in detail each and every type of insult that had been recounted in either camp. Like a healer taking out each thorn one by one, he took out the memories from each and every heart and laid it bare and bleeding before Joseph. Gradually as the people became more used to the renunciations, the crimes recounted became worse. Tears flowed as families remembered their sufferings in the reprisals and counter reprisals. The holocaust of hearts was now taking place.

To a fanfare of bugles and a roll of drums the brazen snake with the head of Jesus was raised aloft and then slowly placed in the hands of Joseph. With their arms crossed over their hearts the two kings kissed the image and then embraced. A mighty cheer echoed and re-echoed up and down the valley.

After the kings' came the turn of the faithful, who slowly moved up the valley to kiss the image.

Mulfra had the good sense to not make the ceremony long. The smell of the cooking came drifting up the valley. A popular song to the dawn drew the ceremony to an end as the hungrier elements of the crowd already were beginning to edge their way sturdily towards the source of the smells.

By the time the Kings were seated at the high table, groups were milling round the various cooking pots and roasting spits. A bronze gong signaled Joseph to shout out the grace and another gong signaled the start of the melee. The noise reached a crescendo and then died down as each began to have his fill.

Silence rained down on the party as hungry bellies were eagerly filled. When it was seen that there would be food and drink in plenty, the party became more relaxed, conversation returned, and then laughter and merriment as drink began to have its effect on bodies wearied by days of discomfort on the march.

As the afternoon wore on snores interspersed the rattle of the feasting; bodies lay idly chewing on some item of food as they basked in the afternoon sun.

Evening came, the benches and tables were pushed to one side, and the music and dancing started. First the troubadours, to set the mood, and then slowly as shyness gradually dissolved, the tribes began to dance. Groups of young men, clinging together for solidarity, eyed the new girls and made comments about them. Self-conscious guffaws occasionally emanated from one or other of the groups. The girls excitedly exchanged impressions as they viewed the young stags walking up and down the field. Some of the more daring would sweep past close to them on the pretext of collecting something, sweeping their victim with a flashing sidelong glance.

It was at this point that Eleanor, in full command of the situation, grabbed one of the Minoth young bucks and pushed him towards one of the Chun damsels. She had spotted him as a likely suitor for one of her cousins, during her stay with the Minoths. In order to mask her stratagem she also pushed others of both Chun and Minoth towards each other. Soon they were mingling freely in animated conversation and wild dancing, as each stag sought to show off his dancing prowess in front of his doe. Laughter and squeals regaled the evening.

Meanwhile Joseph placed himself at the edge of the dancing, gathering together the maimed children and the mentally defective, making sure that they were fed and entertained. He even danced with some of them, much to the affectionate amusement of the mothers, who appreciated the attention given to their neglected children.

Here was a respected foreigner in some strange way giving love and attention, as though they were his own children. Joseph did this because he knew that his master had done the same in Palestine and also because he was disturbed and needed their protection, not only from the more excitable young girls of the flock but also from Eleanor.

Eleanor was dressed in Royal attire; her hair had been carefully prepared by her maids and was interwoven with river pearls. Her necklace, diadem and bangles and amulets were of pure gold; the blend of animal skin and cloth was stunning. Her hair shone like the setting sun behind her, and he was hesitant to meet her.

Eleanor for her part understood the dilemma of her little teacher and was not insulted by it. She looked at the slightly misshapen man dancing with the little ones, a cultural misfit, out of place in the seeming order of things. And yet he had brought a light to this realm which would never be extinguished.

This light would pass from person to person until this realm would be but a sea of dancing light, illuminating eyes and giving warmth to the heart.

"Dear Jesus," Eleanor whispered, "I renounce now and forever even the thought of marriage; and I shall from now on give myself, whole and entire, to the most neglected in this realm. Please help me to carry out this resolution because without you, I cannot." Looking at Joseph: "Please, Lord, allow me to die after this man so that he will not die alone in a foreign land."

"Come here my most beloved daughter and sit by me." Eleanor smiled and swept over to her father and kissed him tenderly. She had found somebody safe to kiss, and at this moment she wanted to kiss everyone who came near her. Her heart felt as light as a feather.

"Before you say anything, my daughter, I want to say something to you.

"Do not despise that man over there," pointing to Joseph, "mark my words he is the bearer of something wonderful; more wonderful than we can imagine. It is not a thing we can touch or even describe and explain, but he is going to change us all. Like light shining through quartz which reveals every beauty and yet every flaw, he can go down into the recesses of men's souls. He is a changer of men because he can reach the very core of their being. Such men are either very dangerous, or wondrous in their dealings with men."

"Papa, I love you more than any other person, but there is someone more wonderful than you. He offered his life for us and for our wrong-doings and has come to this world to bring all souls to everlasting peace. I am going to tell you slowly about him and what he wants us to do on this Earth. Listen and be faithful to his commands because he is the King of all kings and his will must be obeyed. In return he will love us and eventually make his home in our hearts so that they will be filled with his Love. Don't ask me how. I cannot answer, but he has revealed this to that man over there. Now do you think that I could ever despise him?"

"Married love is selfish, my dear, especially in men. It takes a lifetime to grow in generosity. It takes a very wise man to see the folly of sensual love and seek the love of person, the love of hearts united. With your mother it was easy because she was the best friend I ever had, but few are blest with such goodness."

"Papa, I have no intention of marrying. Once is enough, and I do not want the memory of my husband mingled with another. The shadows of my memory are in sharp relief, and I do not want them blurred. You chose wisely when you picked my husband, but I do not want to test fate by giving you another chance. This time you may not be so wise and I want no folly to tarnish your gray hairs." With this Eleanor caressed her father's head and kissed him again.

Dauwid ap Chun seemed to purr like a cat with contentment. What a sweet ending to his years, peace with the Minoths and the love and blessing of his daughter.

"But what about that man over there? Do you love him?"

"Papa, I believe that that man over there is married to God; and God is a jealous lover. Would you be so daring as to tempt fate? The spirit that comes out of him comes because of his covenant with God, and God has shown him special favor; he is a lover of all because he loves God with his all.

"Do you understand that, Papa?"

"I think I do. At first I loved your mother because she was fair and beautiful; later I loved her because of her kindliness and love. Men are greedy and selfish; they always want something. Later I loved her for who she was, someone I knew, understood, and wanted to be with. She had been at my side through all the joys and blows of living and I did not have to explain . . . not to her.

"Life is now empty without her. Since she died, life has never been the same. Now I am the counsellor, and in that I seek consolation. Man always seeks self, directly or indirectly. I suppose only God can seek others because he must be complete in himself. He must give himself to others through others.

"I repeat what I said earlier, Eleanor. Do not underestimate that man. He is going to change more than a kingdom or two. When you are able, send us some teachers. We shall receive them worthily. Now be off, my dear. I have some kingly business to attend to with King Minas ap Minoth."

The following two days were spent in sports, plays, and competitions with the inevitable dancing in the evening stretching far into the night.

Joseph and Mulfra staged many biblical plays and the story-tellers also recounted the stories and explanations given by the prophets.

On the final day, early in the morning, the tired parties left together for their own kingdoms. Many a Chun escorted a

Minoth back to their homestead and vice versa with the blessing and praise of their parents. There is nothing like a few marriages to seal a covenant.

Eleanor supervised the clearing of the feast and the giving of the left-over food to the poor and elderly, and life flowed quickly back to normal. With the coming of winter, lessons began in earnest. She fully intended to send teachers to her father.

# CHAPTER 17

# ✣ The Coming
of the Romans

The battles in the east against the Belgian intruders had not been going well. Slowly one by one the forts had fallen along the coast, as the Belgian settlers moved slowly west.

Fresh battles against the Romans on the continent had sent many refugees across the channel, and these in turn had put fresh pressure on the British. These newcomers were desperate men and fought with determination brought on by calamity and the abandonment of their homeland. They were turning the tide of battle.

As the defeat of battle began to look as though it might turn into a rout, the United Kingdoms of the British in the west decided to call in the Romans as allies. Some of these troops were ferried to the Fal and even Morvah's ships were hired for the purpose.

Joseph made sure he got a generous price for his ships. In war, money is no object and it is a seller's market. Morvah's and Joseph's wealth increased greatly during this period: Joseph immediately invested in books, writing materials and a stone library with generous space and light. He designed it according to his own favorite rabbinical library in Caesaria, modern and with Greek and Roman architectural influence. The Roman occupation had given him easy access to Marsalla, and he also had by chance made contact with a small Christian community there. It was here that the death of his family had been confirmed. The entire family had suddenly disappeared from Jerusalem, and nobody knew the reason. Speculation was that they had been kidnapped and killed. Joseph did not enlighten anybody by explaining the reason: for his own safety he chose not to reveal his identity. He had also found out that orders had gone out for his arrest to all the provinces of Rome. Such a wide dispersion of the order meant that Rome did not know where he was. Azim had done well. His chances of arrest were remote, provided he was cautious.

The Christian community in Marsalla treated him with some suspicion since they knew that Christ's followers did not come from the north, especially one dressed in skins. Israel had always had its fair share of heretics. Was this man one who had fled in earlier times? His knowledge of Christianity was pitiful. Joseph was always in a hurry and never had time to stay long in Marsalla.

Yet he was curious and asked for their writings of the New Faith, offering to pay to have them transcribed, even paying for extra copies for their own use. As a community they were very poor, their following mostly slaves, and they had difficulty with the language.

They looked forward to his visits, his witty use of the Hebrew tongue, and his stories of the north. He had absorbed Celtic imagery into the Hebrew language. The dramatic pause for effect and the rhythmic and sometimes arrhythmic use of phrasing, were new to the ancient rhythms of Hebrew; and he enjoyed the dramatic novelty introduced into his own language. The Hebrew carried the distinct flavor of Morvah and Mulfra although his listeners were not to know it.

Joseph thought it prudent not to let them know who he was, and this prudence in part had caused their suspicion. The law of Rome had a very long memory; and he knew the dangers of careless gossip, especially if he told them that Christ had appeared to him after his death on the cross. Such things were bound to get about, and one of the Roman spies would be bound to report such an extraordinary event even to cynical Roman officials. Roman administration was thorough and often cruel in its defense of Roman order. Enemies and outlaws could only expect Roman justice.

It was while he was away in Marsalla that Eleanor received unexpected guests. A Roman officer called at her compound and presented her with an order. Her house was to be confiscated for New Roman quarters. She was given one day to leave. Her belongings were put onto a donkey cart, and she was ordered out of the area but minus her jewelry.

As she was leaving she could hear the Commander's wife and daughters arguing as to who should wear which item. Beyond the gate of the compound she was on her own. Later she found out that her husband's relatives had connived at the scheme, partly to save sequestration of their own property. Her servants were ordered to serve their new masters since they knew how to administer the house.

Eleanor led her donkey slowly down the hill. She kissed her belongings as though they were the body of Jesus going to the tomb. She kissed the head of her little donkey and the mark of the cross in the fur on the animal's back. Did God not ordain from all eternity the sign of the cross on the back of every donkey? She had not noticed it before, but the sight of it and the realization of its significance gave a bittersweet aroma to the confused spirit inside her.

She made her way automatically to Blonwen's house. Morvah was in Marsalla with Joseph.

Near the house the cart stopped and news, which travels fast in the village, had gone ahead of her. Some already knew of the impending disaster, especially the carters, who had overheard orders days before.

One of the rough boys of the village, son of one of the transport men, threw a lump of earth at her, hitting her on the neck. This unexpected humiliation caused her to burst into tears.

The boy laughed amused at his daring in being the first to 'stand up' against this fine lady now brought down to Earth. Blonwen, who had watched her descent down the hill with growing emotion, and had seen her kisses, in some strange womanly way had grasped intuitively their significance.

"Shame! shame!" Blonwen rushed out. Her copious body smothered Eleanor. She could barely see over the tops of her tears, like a man tied to a prow seeing the top of the water as the ship hovers in deep water and stays for the moment before sinking.

Blonwen's heart sank at that moment, and she grasped Eleanor to prevent herself from drowning in sorrow.

"Shame! shame!"

Blonwen had not the gift of words like her husband, but the tenor of the cry made up for lack of sophistication by the simplicity of the emotion.

Eleanor swam in it like a duck around her solitary duckling. She had come down from the hill in two senses. She was no longer the aloof lady of the fort, but had come down to be among her neighbors. She would now find her true friends; and Blonwen, dear precious Blonwen, was one of them.

The loss of her treasures was somewhat of a relief, because she had been wondering how to get rid of them without offending her kinsfolk; and now the problem had been solved for her in one quick swoop.

Blonwen brought Eleanor into the house to clean the mud stain from her neck. She then did what she often used to do with one of her distraught elder daughters when rejected in love. She started to brush Eleanor's hair, weaving some of her trinkets in and putting her simple jewelry onto her.

When she had finished she took a simple bronze mirror and showed Eleanor her handiwork. It was difficult for Eleanor not to smile.

She looked awful.

Poor Blonwen had such little taste.

Eleanor turned to her. "Blonwen, aristocracy is a question of personality, not of dress or lineage; and compared to you I don't deserve even to be your serving maid."

A few more tears and then a smile and Blonwen went to prepare something for the evening meal. They talked for a little, and then Eleanor took off her trinkets, asking if she could borrow them when she needed them, and then retired.

She left the doorway and stoutly climbed the ladder into the loft, feeling carefully in the hay for any nest of eggs buried there. She did not fancy a cold plunge in the pond to wash off any yolk. She slept soundly.

Much to the delight of both of them, Morvah and Joseph returned next day. While Blonwen blurted out the news, Joseph insisted that Eleanor move into his house while he sought accommodation with an aged widow at the end of the village.

It took an angry command of Joseph finally to persuade Eleanor to move. Meanwhile Morvah was on the move. He collected five of his sailors, noted for their simple devotion and great strength, and led them to the transport end of the village. Joseph, Blonwen, and Eleanor sat apprehensively as the noise and hubbub rose and fell from that end of the village. There was no crashing and banging of objects, and so Blonwen was assured that the proceedings were all only verbal.

Morvah, red of face, demanded that the culprit be brought forward. A small crowd of the villagers gathered around as Morvah proclaimed Eleanor's virtues, the kindness she had shown to all, and now the terrible ingratitude and humiliation. There was little trouble in finding the culprit. The expression of fear and guilt lay stretched over his face.

He was brought to the center of the group.

What proceeded from then on can best be described as a verbal flogging. Those who had known Eleanor, particularly those who had been down the mine, dramatically recounted how they had been helped by her.

Some had to pause as the tension of the moment deprived them of speech. The crowd were moved, and the boy had nowhere to hide, nor was he able even to cover his face. He buried his face between his knees and covered the back of his head with his hands, but still the chastisement came seeping through his fingers into his ears.

Back at Blonwen's house the noise seemed to die down; then there was silence for some time, and then finally a timid knock at the door.

Blonwen went to the door, and then turned and indicated to Eleanor that it was for her.

When Eleanor went to the door she found the boy on his knees with a tray in his hands and goblets of horn and bronze.

The look of hard defiance had gone, and the soft eyes of a young boy had returned.

Eleanor couldn't make out what he said, and she didn't want to increase his humiliation by pressing him to speak out more loudly.

She thanked him for the present, took it and placed it on a stool behind her, then resting the boys face in her hands, she whispered. "When you marry, treat your wife with kindliness and respect. Remember what I have told you."

After the little ceremony, the boy got up and ran to the woods to his favorite hiding place to be alone and lick his wounds.

# CHAPTER 18

## ❧ The New School

After house moving had been completed and a new maid found for Eleanor, Joseph called together his students.

"Until this moment, your instruction has been because of the kindness of Eleanor. Now we are all poor, and such tuition cannot be afforded any more.

"From now on you have to decide whether you value what you have learned and whether you want to continue. From now on you will have to pay. Go home and think about it, and in two days time come to be enrolled."

Two days later it was with some trepidation that Eleanor and Joseph walked towards the library, but what a sight met their eyes as they turned the corner!

A long line of people waited for them, each with a struggling child at the end of their arm.

News had gone out that education could be bought and many purchasers were there waiting for them.

Eleanor and Joseph had not realized how much the education of the intelligent, privileged few had been envied by the neighborhood.

Now education had, by force of circumstances, become a market commodity.

Joseph did a quick count of heads, and then he stood in the doorway of the library. "Thank you my friends for coming. We had not expected so many. Nobody shall be refused an education, but we need a little time to re-organize"

And so it was: Joseph took his best and oldest students and offered them jobs as teachers in his new school as well as opportunities for deeper study. They all proved excited and willing. Some had found difficulty in getting time off from their duties to attend to the new learning, and here was the opportunity for both learning and employment.

Rooms and barns were rented; some parents who could little afford the fees could make payment in food, fuel, or building materials, or in offering themselves as hired labor in the school.

Over the coming months, more came to join the school from outlying villages while various groups sought accommodation in the village. Many of the needy gained a new means of livelihood by offering room and board to students.

Over the next few years the school grew rapidly, and even the Romans began to send their children to the school as the families began to follow their men-folk from Gaul to Britain.

The school became firmly established and thrived.

# CHAPTER 19

## ⚶ A Roman Incident

It was just an ordinary day, uneventful, full of the same daily routine; as usual Joseph was distracted and busy. Trade with Gaul had increased considerably due to the influx of the Romans and so profits had increased. All this needed careful bookkeeping. Work at the school had increased phenomenally, and Joseph was still tutoring the most advanced students in preparation for their role as future teachers of teachers.

Other villages, out of their existing orbit, were clamoring for schools to be started and were making all kinds of tempting offers, provided that a new school would start in their village first. Parents could see changes in their children and so did their neighbors and relatives from the remoter villages.

Many began to rely on their children for writing and reading of letters, some even from relatives in Gaul, who had married into families there.

Some of Joseph's messengers to Gaul had found romance and had settled in Gaul, but still kept in written contact with their homeland. This was new and novel and caused excitement.

Joseph was in a shop that made parchment; he was distracted and hardly noticed a Roman soldier who had entered behind him.

"I need a piece of parchment large enough to take this writing," Joseph said. It was a quotation from one of the prophets.

"That is Hebrew writing," said the soldier, grabbing the scroll.

"Yes"

"Are you a Jew?"

Joseph smiled, "I am a Jew who loves Jesus Christ."

Joseph only felt the blow two days later when he awoke in his bed, with a moist cloth on his head.

Eleanor was sitting by the window embroidering tapestry. "A centurion saved your life. He stopped a soldier from killing you and has asked to see you when you regain consciousness."

Joseph nodded his head until the pain stopped him. "In a few days' time, I think," remarked Eleanor, familiar with blows to the head.

"You must have the constitution of an ox, since not many people recover from two days' unconsciousness. They usually get other things wrong with them and their breathing stops. An old nurse told me to always keep unconscious people on their side and their head slightly lower than their body. It seems to have worked in your case. You started sleeping more naturally about half a day ago."

Joseph realized she had slept little during his sojourn and was grateful.

After a few days Joseph could sit up although he felt a weakness down one side and his speech had developed a slight slur.

"So you love Jesus Christ," said the centurion as he entered the room and sat down by Joseph's chair. "And how would you know about Jesus Christ?"

"I met him."

"So have I, *mirabile dictu*, but only as a boy. My father was also a centurion and a friend of Israel. I overheard your remark as I was passing and heard the blow. He is one of my men and will be coming to see you later . . .

"Do not be too hard on him. His entire family was killed by religious zealots, as was my father. My mother brought me up in the Christian faith, and when I became a priest, she returned to relatives in Rome. She works now in the palace of Nero: so she is safe, thank God . . .

"Bitterness is a terrible thing. It can turn a man insane. My Christian religion forbids me to hate. I am a Christian priest 'according to the order of Melchisedech.' I believe that even Melchisedech was a gentile, and so here I am. My name is Demas. I am an engineer for the Roman legion and I have the status of Centurion."

"My whole family was killed by the Romans," Joseph replied, "and Jesus appeared to me after his death on the cross. He promised he would come and stay with me before my physical death, and I really am not worried about danger from anyone."

"Have you been baptized?"

"No, I did not have time to hear John the Baptist preach."

"I am talking of Christian baptism, the baptism of Jesus Christ."

"I heard reports that some of Christ's disciples were imitating John the Baptist, but that is all."

"My friend, this baptism makes us all children of God, no matter what tribe or nation we come from. We all become equally children of God, as brothers and sisters to each other and sharing in the almighty Trinity of God the Father, God the Son, and God the Holy Spirit. The new family of God includes all nations, tribes, and races, united in Christ, our Redeemer."

"I never thought I would ever, ever, hear words like that from a Roman" said Joseph with a twinkle in his eye. "Piety to their father, yes, but after that the children fight like tigers over the inheritance."

"We shall all inherit a kingdom, and so why bother?" replied the soldier, entering into the humor.

"Eleanor, would you like to be my sister?"

"Does it pay better than a servant?" smiled Eleanor. "Sounds as if you want my services on the cheap."

"I would consider it a great honor if you would be my sister, and I am being serious."

"Well then, let us find out what all this means first, shall we? I am sure our centurion friend has a lot of explaining to do. The word Trinity sounds strange to me, and so does baptism."

"It will take almost a year of instruction. And you can be received into the Church on the anniversary of Christ's glorious resurrection: if you are willing."

Joseph, who never did anything halfway, after a few lessons went around the area, bringing all his teachers, all his pupils and anybody who had received instruction from him. Above all he brought Morvah, Blonwen, and Mulfra, and his Druid, Bard and Ovate companions, to the new instruction. To those who did not speak Roman he acted as translator, as did Eleanor with the womenfolk.

All this meant an increasing burden on their existing work-load, but they worked with increasing urgency.

With startling rapidity Joseph grasped the full meaning of the New Covenant, a personal covenant—that God would be their Father.

All the previous covenants of the Law and the Prophets rushed through Joseph's mind as he heard the new words of Christ, and waves of excitement passed over him as he sat in the benches along with his fellow classmates.

He became jokingly known as a troublesome disturber as he rushed in with Old Testament quotations to support the words of the teacher, his mind racing ahead of his speech, and now with a slight lisp which made his voice comical.

He was a new, young, excited pupil, in love with the new learning.

"You see. It has all been prefigured by Christ from the day of Adam and Eve," he often used to shout.

Hoots of mockery came floating down the gallery, as students enjoyed Joseph's new role as pupil.

# CHAPTER 20

## ⚜ The Eucharist

"Do you remember, Joseph, when Jesus said 'I shall stay with you before your physical death?'" said Demas in one of his lessons.

"Can I ever forget it?"

"Do you realize what he meant by that?"

"That I would see him again before I die."

"No, not necessarily, something better. You will . . . receive . . . him before you die. The bread and wine of Melchizedech in the Old Law has become the Body and Blood of Christ in the New Law. When I perform the sacrifice of the New Law, I transform the bread and wine into the real Body and Blood of Christ, who remains hidden under the appearance of bread and wine. I eat his Body."

A thud of disappointment hit Joseph.

It sounded like a broken promise. He had told everyone that Jesus would walk with him physically before he died.

His whole being had been sustained through all the difficult moments of life in Britain by the thought that eventually he would have the companionship, the advice and the love and interest of Christ, walking with him as they discussed new developments and projects for the work in Britain.

Christ would be able to do in Britain what he had failed to do in Jerusalem. Britain would, in some way, be a place to recoup forces, to gather new recruits, for a renewed assault on Rome; catching it where it least expected it—from the north.

The enormously rough, crude and resilient forces of the north, once inspired, led, and trained would become a force mightier than any of Rome. Their toughness, their sheer numbers, their breeding rate, their love of children and family, their loyal family bonds, their simple life, would make them ideal for a mighty army.

He had seen the fighting qualities of the Gauls and had heard by repute of the fighting qualities of the tribes north and east of the Rhine. Not even the Roman legions dared to cross the Rhine for anything bigger than a punitive raid.

The Romans knew they could be surrounded and crushed by sheer numbers. The people from the north had a much tougher lifestyle than the Romans. The Roman army was still tough and disciplined, but even the army was finding it harder to get Roman recruits ready to put up with hardships and were beginning to recruit non-Romans. A good number of Phoenicians were in the Roman army in Britain.

And now this Greek talk of the Eucharist—a love feast— Agapé.

"Cannibalism is repugnant to the Jewish religion. It is a thing of the unbelievers, of dark satanic sects," Joseph retorted, doubtfully.

"These are the words of Jesus himself: 'Unless you eat of my flesh and drink of my blood, you shall not have life in you,'" responded Demas.

Joseph shrugged, turned to the class and remarked "Anybody any ideas?" He wanted to draw attention away from himself to allow him time to think.

He was profoundly disturbed, and feelings of rejection were beginning to foment inside of him.

"I really can't see any problem," perked a bright-eyed youngster from the back of the class.

He had reached the adulthood of childhood, precocious for his years, before the emotional turmoil of adolescence could add obscurity to the clarity of his mind.

"If I were to give meat to a cow it would die. If I were to give hay to a pig it would wither and die. Each animal must have the food proper to its kind.

"Now since we are to be children of God, both body and soul, then the only food proper to us for our journey through life is the body and spirit of Jesus himself. Only his food can suffice for the journey of our life to Heaven."

"And Elijah took the scone of the Lord and walked forty days and forty nights until he reached Horeb," muttered Joseph.

Joseph was silent; he afterwards went to the barn where a Christian altar had been erected and prayed for many hours, turning over in his mind all the implications of what he had heard.

Over many days he walked along the cliff top, suddenly stopping and shouting out something in Hebrew and then turning back to his thoughts.

# CHAPTER 21

# ≷ A Moment of Decision

Autumn had come and the nights were coming earlier and earlier. The sky that night was a fiery glow on the horizon. The sea was as calm as crystal, and Joseph walked up and down on the cliff top.

He had walked up and down that little path so often that he didn't even have to look for the way. He knew it by instinct; every tree, every bush and hillock and crack in the path. That is why he liked it there. He could walk up and down thinking without the distraction of finding his way.

But Joseph was lost, swimming in a cloud of lost dreams. His feet and body were in contact with the hard reality of Earth. The cold of the evening cut through his fur clothing and touched the surface of his flesh with its clammy hand.

The sky was a clear relic of an autumn day which had seemed, in its brightness, more like summer; but now the winter smell of earth and water touched his nostrils, and all the plants and trees seemed stilled in the quietness of death waiting for winter. He was alone with his thoughts and the night sky.

"Oh Lord, Destroyer of dreams and aspirations, who can know your mind? We are presumptuous to presume to know your plans."

"Have you lost interest in Jerusalem? Have you stopped loving your people? Does your disgraceful death preclude us from your promise? Yet what chance could we mortals have if God were not to keep his promises? Who could endure? The covenant you made with Adam to be your child, made in your own image and likeness, broken by man, not by God . . .

"The renewed covenant with Noah . . . that God would be with him and his family. The covenant of circumcision, made with Abraham that Israel would be his people, that the children of Abraham would be numberless, like the stars in the heavens."

Joseph stopped and looked up at the sky.

There was no moon, and the sky was a mass of twinkling light. The farthest were so faint and numerous that they seemed like milk cast onto a sea of timelessness.

"We cannot breed that much, oh Lord. Never can the children of Israel produce so many, unless we are to be on this earth for an infinity."

Joseph continued his walk.

"And the Messiah is to be of the line of David.

"I believe you to be the Messiah, Jesus . . . entering Jerusalem on a donkey as the prophets foretold; a man burdened with grief; a man who took upon his own sacred flesh the burden of our sins and wickedness. . . . The sins of Israel, oh Lord . . . or the sins of mankind? . . .

"Your new covenant, then, is not with Israel only, our nation, but with all nations, all made brothers and sisters by baptism. These are the words of Demas. You are to be the Father of many nations and you will be our God. You died for all mankind, oh Lord. Your death on the cross redeemed the whole of mankind. . . . But what of this new covenant, Lord? Demas tells us . . . that in the Eucharist you are crucified again for us in an un-bloody way. You present again the death and resurrection of Golgotha . . .

"When our tribe would walk between the lumps of meat along with an allied tribe, signifying a covenant, betrayal would mean that the treacherous tribe would lose even the right to choose their own death. They lost all rights to existence. You put a wonderful thing into the head of that child in the lesson with Demas. 'Thou whose glory above the heavens is chanted by the mouth of babes and infants, thou has founded a bulwark because of thy foes, to still the enemy and the avenger' Ps 8:2.

"From the beginning of time did you write those lines for me, oh Lord; 'To still the enemy and the avenger.'

"Sun, wind and rain make grass; grass becomes cow when consumed by such; cow becomes human when eaten; each taken into a higher form of life. And then with this new covenant, man eats thee and becomes what he eats, God; a son or daughter of God. Has thy body become the bridge between fallen man and God?

"Not just man but the whole of creation has been rejoined to the Godhead through thy Body and Blood, Soul and Divinity.

"Adam ate the apple to become 'like unto God,' and the apple of self-assertion fell to the ground rotten. Thou in reply hast indeed made us Gods, joined us to thy Godhead, through thy sacrifice on the cross . . .

"Because of our betrayal you became priest and victim, choosing the worst of all deaths . . . to establish a new covenant with us. The covenant to be the children of God. To raise us to the Trinitarian Godhead. To make us Gods, sons and daughters of God. Is it possible, Lord, to receive a greater gift? And the reason? . . . Our sins. What an absurdity of love!

"Since you rose from my tomb—my family tomb—lift me too, oh sweet Jesus, from the darkness of my own wickedness. . . . Lift this burden of doubt from me.

"Oh Lord, I grieve to despair. Why have you guided me here to this Godforsaken place, if not for some purpose? If it is not to re-establish the might and power of Jerusalem, then why?"

When the fallen warriors of the chief Celtic god were immersed in his cauldron, they gained new life. They passed from death to life

Your chalice, your Grail, shall be the cauldron of new life. When we drink your blood, we shall redeem our fallen natures into the new life of the Trinity, creation given new life by your blood shed from the cross for us.

Joseph began to pray in Latin even though to pray in that language was repugnant to him as the language evoked hatred in his heart from bitter memory. Somehow he had to try to forgive his enemies, as Christ had done, in order to try and reduce the hatred that still remained in his heart.

"In tuum pretiosum sanguinem immerge me, clementissime Jesus
Ut ex tuo calice bibam
Da mihi novum cordem
Ex inordinati cogitationis ira duc me per tuas vias.

(In your precious blood, oh dearest Jesus, immerse me,
So that I may drink from your Grail,
Give me a new heart,
And lead me in your ways, and from the anger of
  inordinate feelings.)

"This Grail shall replace the cauldron of the Celtic gods," murmured Joseph at the end of his Latin prayer.

Joseph prayed until the dawn rose over the mountains and lit the dew on his clothing like a myriad of stars, like precious jewels, reflecting the light more perfectly than the finest jewels of Arabia. And the birds charmed and caressed him with their music.

Joseph felt contented.

"In your own good time, Lord, you shall enlighten me, because you are good and have pity on the stupidity of men."

Joseph did not feel sleepy at all after the sleeplessness of the night, but felt strangely refreshed.

# CHAPTER 22

## ⚜ Demas

"You think too much, Joseph. You pray with the mind, but the heart must take part also. To pray well, we have to conquer hate. . . . Christ has entered a new covenant more wonderful because it is a personal covenant with you and me . . .

"God's love has always been personal, with Demas, with Eleanor, and with Joseph. The testament of the Prophets is a vast teaching, preparing us for the coming of Christ, for a new Covenant.

"The conquest of Christ is not over nations or against armies, but the conquest of hearts, one by one; with the poorest, with the richest, with Roman, Greek, Jew, British. . . . Our love of God is to be personal, in the intimacy of our hearts. Jerusalem is in your heart Joseph, as it is in mine.

"We are to carry in our hearts now the living sign and symbol of Christ crucified. We are to give our hearts the light and warmth of the Resurrection, and we are to give them the heart beat of the Holy Spirit.

"We are to carry the Trinity in our hearts so that we be light and warmth to others. Ours is to be a conquest of disinterested love. Our armor is to be our virtues, and our sword, the Holy Spirit. This love will be mightier than the clamor of a thousand armies because it shall have the stillness and might of a gentle wind."

From that day on, Joseph began to prepare for the homecoming of the Lord into his heart. . . . He was content.

## ELEANOR

To Eleanor, the Eucharist was never a problem. Her mind rose like a falcon, grasped its meaning, and then swooped back to Earth very contented.

Men are often slow and laborious in their reasoning, while women can grasp things immediately.

Her love was thrilled and somehow reached its completion with the revelation of the Eucharist—and so it must be true.

She was much before Joseph in awaiting, with eagerness, the coming of Easter.

## THE WATERS OF THE WELL

The first wave of Baptisms and receptions of the Eucharist was a relatively quiet affair—Eleanor, Joseph, Mulfra and most of the first class, Morvah and family.

Not so the second wave one year later.

The first wave of missionaries swept out almost from the first day like a rip tide round a headland in a stormy wind.

They fanned out into the villages forming small eddy currents in each village inlet.

Long winter months of instruction by the thin light of oil lamps and winter fire in the village hall.

Parents listening with their children and village chiefs pondering with their elders over these mighty questions.

Some Druids objected, even when Mulfra came to them. Some left, especially those who connected with dark spirits and continued to practice their dark arts, deeper in the forests and in the more remote villages. Some, however, exposed their practices to the priest and revealed their secrets. They burned their vessels and accoutrements.

As Passover, Easter, and the British Spring Festival coincided, it was agreed to retain the symbol of fire in the Easter Dawn Celebration, a feast precious to the British.

A huge fire was lit at the end of the "valley of the meetings."

Mulfra presided over the ceremonies.

At the appropriate moment the rear torches were lit and the wave of light swept down the valley, symbol of the coming of Christ as the light of the World. Joseph shouted out to the crowd before the Baptism "Do you renounce all evil spirits?"

"We do!" came the shout.

"I can't hear you!," claimed Joseph, eager for dramatic repetition.

"We do!" cried the crowd.

"I can't hear you!" shouted Joseph eager for the triple assertion of Peter. At that moment, along with the shout, three shafts of spears whistled past his head and thudded into a wooden pig's head which still adorned one of the podium posts. Joseph then thought it wise to leave the rest to Mulfra, who directed the crowd to the pond.

There was a general scramble as people rushed and pushed to get into the water. Some whose bodies probably had seldom touched water since babyhood squealed at the cold, as they were baptized.

Babies and the aged and the sick were baptized with water pored on their heads from bronze bowls, each person being wiped carefully afterwards by clean white towels, boiled and prepared with fullers earth and scented plant extracts.

The first Eucharist was received in total silence.

Only the crackle of the torches broke the silence. The astrologer Ovates had fixed the position of the cross, so that the dawn sun rose from below and behind, until the shadow of the cross was cast down the valley.

The crowds gradually left, shivering but refreshed by the ordeal. The fire revived many for the journey home. "Anything of value must be suffered for," voiced some as they wended their way home.

Mulfra remarked to Joseph as they too walked home in the dawn: "Next year we must organize the baptism better. They became too cold, particularly the little ones. I like the idea of the bronze bowls and the towels."

## VILLAGE LIFE

Merriment and humor seemed to seep into the villages with the increasing number of baptisms.

People seemed to talk and gossip more freely and less guardedly and feasting became more frequent. The bards were busy creating new music for the new teaching under the encouragement of Joseph and Mulfra; as well as new plays for the traveling theatres, the players of which moved from village to village.

The soldier who had attacked Joseph became a Christian, and Joseph was his god-father.

Councils of elders were established to settle disputes over land, houses, grazing rights, and inheritance, whose judgments were final, an innovation brought in by Dauwid and Minas as a safeguard against a return to feuding; and this system was copied by other kingdoms in the vicinity.

'The rule of right to replace the rule of might' became a slogan of the people.

# CHAPTER 23

## ✥ A New Visitor

Spring was always a nice time of the year in the Fal kingdom; bright blue crystal clear skies, clean fresh breezes, and the new leaves on the trees sparkling in green cleanliness. Here and there a fountain of color rose from the ground in floral cascade as the bushes displayed their loveliness. Joseph, as usual, was in a hurry to meet a new ship in the harbor to see if it contained any cargo for himself.

"Somebody is asking for a person who sounds like you," a sailor hurrying home to his family remarked, as he passed him on his way to the village. Joseph scrutinized the crew and the few passengers milling on the jetty, but couldn't see anyone he recognized. The captain pointed a finger in his direction as he spotted Joseph coming down the path and a young man detached himself from the group and walked towards him. He spoke in Aramaic.

"Are you Joseph?"

"Yes."

"From Jerusalem?"

Joseph hesitated for a moment and then said "yes."

"Did you escape from Callistus?"

Now Joseph really did pause this time and looked at the young man. The hesitancy gave the game away. The young man looked composed, clear eyed and of fresh complexion, of the type that could indicate either simple innocence or dark and devious malice.

"Why do you ask?"

"Because I am looking for my father. I am Joseph of Arimathea's son. My mother has sent me."

"Is her name Rebecca?"

"Yes, and I'm David."

"But the whole family was killed by Callistus, Joseph was the only one who escaped."

"No, Mary spoke to the wife of Pilate, and the order was rescinded."

Joseph suddenly felt very, very, tired. He wanted to go and lie down. He didn't say anything but then suddenly burst into tears.

Slowly they both walked up the hill to Eleanor's house, Joseph in silence. He would occasionally turn to his son and try to say something, but the effort only caused more tears and he gave up trying.

Eleanor was very worried when she saw Joseph's face at the doorway. She thought there had been a re-occurrence of his brain damage. His face looked terrible, and his eyes reddened. His lack of speech worried her even more. She immediately led Joseph to his dwelling and ordered him to lie down. Joseph obeyed without protest. He indicated David to her, and then lay down and almost immediately fell into a deep sleep.

## TALES FROM THE EAST

It was before dawn of the next day when Joseph awoke feeling much better. In fact he was ablaze with curiosity and excitement. He got up, prepared the fire, planned the breakfast, set the table, got things ready, and then checked the breakfast again. Dawn had still not broken. He went outside to await the dawn, went back in to check the breakfast, went into the garden to collect some fresh herbs, went back in the house to check the wine, and went outside again to check the position of the sun. It still hadn't shown itself over the mountain. He walked down the pathways to the village and then to Eleanor's house. The house was in silence, but he noticed a fire was still smoking. She had a visitor. David must be staying there. Selfishly he thought of knocking on the door with some paltry excuse, but decided not to disturb them.

He walked slowly back to his house and sat on the porch. He often enjoyed sitting there when it rained. The porch sheltered him, yet he could hear the rain pattering on the leaves in the garden. He sat there looking at the sky and thanking God in his Infinite Mercy.

"What a nerve you have, oh God! I could never even have thought on this scale. . . . To think . . . that you planned all this from all eternity.

"Nothing is ever by chance. It is always ordained by your holy will. All these years spent on the edge of the world; Christianity at its farthest reach from Jerusalem.

"Why here, oh Lord? There must be a serious reason. But why such interest in a land of swamp, impenetrable dank forest, and bramble? If the brambles and thorns don't cut you to pieces, the swamp will suck you down to the bottomless depths. A few hill folk and fishermen and that is all; no cities, no towns, and no real industry; just a few people, now learning to write in Roman.

"Oh Lord, please give them fine roads, handsome towns, and valleys with beautiful fields and pastures, each town with a house dedicated to you.

"Give them fine ships and commerce and covered markets, paved roads and fountains and spacious gardens that surpass Rome and Athens.

"Give them good libraries and meeting houses and forums and centers of learning. Give them good theater, give them good writers that delight in the knowledge of man and the ways of his soul. Through them, may these people get to know thee, to love thee with all their heart and to love their fellow men with increasing knowledge and understanding."

As Joseph prayed the time seemed to pass more quickly. The sun was well up when he saw fresh smoke coming from the roof of Eleanor's house and he hurried to give his greetings.

"Well you two must have a lot to talk about," said Eleanor. "I am afraid I kept him up late and he has told me lots of things already. You go and have breakfast with him, and I will arrange things at the school."

As they settled down on the leather cushions by the fire, Joseph, as an offering to God, did not question his son until he had eaten well.

Fortunately Joseph had prepared well, for David had a massive appetite. Either the sea voyage, the vigor of youth, or the poor food on the boat had given him a massive appetite.

"Mother sends her greetings, her love, a long letter and a present. She is too weak to make the journey herself and we were not sure we would find you alive."

"It was at Mary's insistence that I came, and she sends her greetings from Ephesus and told me to tell you that because of you this land will have graces and blessings showered upon it, more than the rain that has ever fallen upon it.

"Ruth went with Azim and some others to start the Faith amongst the Parthians. . . . Karen is in upper Egypt and there are very many converted to the Faith in that Region, extending far into Ethiopia. The numbers of converts have reached miraculous proportions . . .

She has started a weaving business and is very successful. She is sometimes able to visit mother in Ephesus during her business trips. We have letters from Ruth to say she is well. The work there is hard. There are many religions there and it creates problems in the understanding of our way. Oh, by the way, father, I am a priest and have been for two years."

"We have another one here already, Demas the centurion. He works with the Roman army on roads and bridges. He will be delighted to have another priest. He hopes to leave the army soon to be a priest full-time. We will employ him at the school. There is so much to be done."

# CHAPTER 24

## ∻ Joyful Days

Joseph took the letter from his son, and the parcel. He hesitated about which to open first. He opted for the parcel to get it out of the way. He would linger over the letter.

The oiled cloth was carefully bound with thongs and the edges of the cloth carefully sealed with wax. He took a knife and eased it carefully down the edges of the cloth. He used the point of the knife to open up the knots of the thongs so as not to damage even the binding. Underneath the cloth lay a cedar box edged in copper and with copper bands of intricate design giving strength. The center band was joined by a clasp which closed the lid. Inside was waxed Egyptian paper, and the aroma of his favorite spiced biscuits issued from beneath their folds. Dried fruit preserved in sugar, each piece carefully wrapped individually, was placed around the edge. Next came the letter.

Joseph carefully broke the wax of the copper cylinder, twisted off the cap and took out the tightly rolled parchment.

Around the edges of the letter were colored decorations of animals and flowers, just as in her letters during their courtship. Some of the animals had amusing expressions and probably related to some passage in the letter. It began:

"*Dearest husband,*

"*I hope and pray that this letter reaches you and that our son gives you all the love and affection that I am not able to give you directly.*

"*I am not strong enough to make the journey, but very much alive and very happy. I am close to Mary and John. What more could we mortals wish for on this earth?*

"*David will be better able to give account of our life here, but it will take some time for him to recount everything. Men are like that and he takes after you in keeping counsel to himself.*

"*He is a lovely boy, and his upbringing has been with the prayers of Mary and her wise counsel.*

"*Mary herself sends greetings and says that you are continuously in her prayers along with those of her Son.*

"*Blessings fall on Britain like the rain from the heavens, since she has made it a special object of her love and attention.*

"*After you left the house, soldiers of Callistus arrested us and took us to prison. Mary interceded for us, and we were released.*

"*When he heard about our arrest, Reuben came over to Callistus and showed him a document, a copy of which he said was already on its way to Rome and would be shown to leading officials if any harm were to come to our family. Callistus became very nervous and decided to accept a bribe similar to the one he would have got from Caiphas.*

"*Reuben also showed a document to Caiphas, and Caiphas readily agreed not to pursue the matter any further . . .*

"*Some days later Callistus came to see me and returned the bribe. He said he would like to give it for the care of lepers. He seemed very nervous.*

"*He said he had joined a crowd listening to the leader of the new religion, and he spoke to him in his own local dialect which he had not revealed to anybody. He had also seen what had happened to Judas.*

"*And here is an interesting bit. Callistus said something quite revealing. He said: 'This new movement will change empires, because it will conquer by curing sicknesses both of body and soul.'*

*"Not bad, eh, Joseph, for a superstitious Roman?*

*"The Apostles decided we should move to Ephesus with Mary.
We sent a message to Marsalla to say we had disappeared, so that
you would not be tempted to return to a certain and horrible death.
There are too many spies in Jerusalem and a well-known person like
yourself certainly would have been betrayed and captured. We did
indeed disappear but only to Ephesus to escape the malice of those in
Jerusalem. We did not tell anyone of our journey except Reuben and
the Apostles. Reuben has kept us supplied with money for all our
needs, including the education of the children."*

The letter then went into detail about events subsequent to
their departure and news of relatives and of their life up to the
time of David's journey to Britain.

Joseph laughed occasionally at the witty comments from
Rebecca in the letter, as his mind pictured the screwed nose and
the wry smile as she penned the phrasing. It took him a long time
to read the letter, and then he read it again, and then glanced at it
a third time, reading some of the passages over again. He then
rolled the letter carefully, unfolded it and then folded it more
tightly to get it into the cylinder.

He placed both items by his bedside, but he was never able to
eat the biscuits. If he raised one to his lips his throat stiffened.
The cinnamon aroma caressed his nostrils, and the memories
came welling up, as though rising from a huge cistern; and he
would put it down again.

He eventually gave them to young children in his classes as
rewards for answering questions correctly. He kept the box on the
small table by his bedside, which he later called his kissing box.

After reading the letter, Joseph walked up and down the
living room of his house for a little while, watching the rain
dripping from the eaves of the porch and bouncing off the leaves,
his heart buffeted by the water like a stone in a stream holding
out against the current.

He eventually turned to his son and said:

"My place is here."

"Mother said you should not return," said David. "It is God's will that you stay in Britain and fulfill your mission."

The matter was never mentioned again by either of them. Even to write would be dangerous since consorting with wanted men carried a cruel death. For a messenger to find them would involve many questions, and each question would increase the chances of betrayal and arrest.

# CHAPTER 25

## ⤙ Beautiful Days

Joseph organized fishing and hunting trips, sometimes, on good days, spending the night in tents under the stars with David, taking fire with them in one of the bronze vessels filled with the mixtures of materials that kept a hot glow during the journey, provided that they occasionally swung it in the air to keep the glow alive. Dry kindling carried with them transformed the glow into vigorous fire, when the time came for fire making.

Joseph enjoyed the fishing trips best, partly because he now found hunting quite exhausting, but mainly because while fishing he could have long conversations with his son; not just during the fishing, but also in the evening by the fire as the bread and the fish cooked in the pit filled with heated stones and covered with turf and leaves.

Joseph not only found out about life in the family at Ephesus but also about deep doctrinal issues of the new Way.

David had been very well trained and answered his enquiries with liberal quotations from the Greek poets and philosophers. The depth of this Greek learning astounded Joseph. God had blessed David with Joseph's intelligence and also the fine features of Rebecca.

As David talked, he often reminded Joseph of Rebecca—the amusing flick of the eyes, the sudden earnest expression and turn of phrase: a message carried in living form, like an invisible dove tossed from the hands of his beloved.

Joseph put David to work almost immediately. Eleanor supervised his learning of British; learning helped by total immersion in the life of the community.

Within six months he was preaching in the language: his written sermons corrected by Eleanor beforehand. David helped with the Roman, Greek, and Hebrew in training the teachers.

David was soon traveling around the villages on his own initiative, accompanied by helpers.

Eleanor sent him to the Chuns, to her father, who was eventually baptized by David's own hand along with many people from the tribe and those of the surrounding middle country.

The baptism was a truly joyous occasion. Eleanor was almost beside herself with joy during the feasting afterwards so that she was hardly able to sit for long, but would get up to busy herself with something or go out to greet visitors she had not met for ages. Her conversation bubbled with laughter. Occasionally she would pretend to hit her father on the shoulder and push him until he rocked from side to side as he made one of his teasing remarks to her.

Dauwid had already made plans for a continuation of the work and had provided fast horses so that David could travel as rapidly as possible between the two communities.

# CHAPTER 26

## ⚛ The Return

For seven seasons David, Demas, and Joseph and the first followers labored; the Church grew.

Joseph noticed that David was growing increasingly restless, and a problem seemed to preoccupy his thoughts. Joseph waited patiently until his son felt able to talk to him about it. The day eventually came. "Father, shall we go for a walk? I want to talk to you."

Joseph was apprehensive and feared the worst—that David was going to leave him.

"Father, we have only two priests and no possibility of getting any more to come and help us. . . . Gaul and Iberia have too few and they have difficulties with the language here. . . . We need priests and other people dedicated to the Lord to expand our work here . . .

"I have thirty men and women willing to make the journey to be trained by the first disciples and I need to go with them. . . . Demas will send others to me later . . .

"There is an important training school at Corinth, founded by Paul and under the supervision of Apollo, a man of very great learning. Priests can cause untold damage if they are not properly trained and allow the ways of the world to creep into their teaching.

"We need to leave soon. I know this will be hard for you, father, but sacrifices made now will bear good fruit in the future."

And so it came to pass. Joseph paid and arranged for guides to take them to Marsalla down the very familiar route and David would arrange the passage to Greece.

Joseph was able to pay for the entire passage for the whole group and to provide them with money for emergencies and for a contribution to the first year of their studies. He would send more money later with others, also called to the dedicated life and sent by Demas.

Joseph's skill in business had brought ample reward in the British trade. He had picked good managers, and trade had expanded.

For Rebecca he had a cross cast in gold and along one side he had written 'Amor vincit omnia'—love conquers all. He had a chain made so that she could wear it around her neck, to remind her of him.

He wrote:

*"Dearest wife, mother of my children, and possessor of my heart,*

*"When I left Jerusalem, I resolved never to think of you again in order to keep my sanity . . .*

*"Now, when David came into my life again, my heart was filled with a bitter joy—joy because I knew that you and all my precious family are alive and that I would be able to spend glorious time with our beloved son; bitterness, because of the apparently wasted years of life away from you and the thought that we shall never meet again this side of eternity.*

*"Yet God's ways are not our ways, and distance and time are of no consequence to people who love God with all their hearts. To love unselfishly is a more refined love and purer, because of the fusing of our hearts in the divine Fire like gold shimmering in a furnace . . .*

*"I shall love you always and wait in hope until we are united once more in heaven and we shall pass eternity together in merriment and good company.*

*"I am glad David is coming to visit you, if only for a short time and I hope he will find you and bring this letter to you.*

*Your loving husband,*
*Joseph."*

The other letters were directed to each of his daughters, and the last part was a long and detailed account of all that had happened since fleeing from Jerusalem. Joseph passed the letter container to David and then led him to the library for a farewell conversation.

"David, a word in your ear." Joseph drew him aside.

"Be very discreet in your journey. Say nothing to others about the reason for your travel, except that it is to seek Roman and Greek learning. Rome is jealous of its empire and Rome represents the peak of development of what is pagan.

"Its boundaries reach almost to the ends of the world, from north to south, east to west; but its foundation stones are pagan . . .

"Christianity will have to remove those stones one by one and replace them with those of Christ. Only Christian stones will make the building lasting. . . . Yet I fear that because of Roman incomprehension, it will look as though we are undermining the edifice. We will be considered a threat.

Rome's reaction will be quick and terrible. Do not be naive. Do not let anybody know what you are doing. Advise them all to be discreet and to talk only in language that the Greeks will understand. Tell them to pray and to study like heroes, but to not be involved in conversions until they are safely back in Britain.

"Praying is more powerful than preaching and their Greek will never reach the sophistication needed in that civilization. . . . Leave conversions to the Greeks. Pray for their success. But devote yourself to study, long hard, detailed, and laborious study.

"If you can obtain Roman citizenship for them, get it and for yourself too. It will provide greater protection. Seek the protection of Roman Law, and come back safely . . .

"To the Romans, Britain is of no significance and they will ignore you. Maybe this is why the Lord has chosen Britain for his work. British Christians, because of their position at the edge of the Empire, their harsh terrain, and their personal austerity may pass unnoticed when the wrath of Rome is enkindled . . .

"Britain is of no significance to the Roman mind; yet we shall keep alive the glow of faith, ready with our kindling when the time is ripe for us to enkindle Europe with the love of Christ.

"Keep safe, David; be wise, discreet and cunning as a fox and like a good dog bring your flock back safely. Make this training of the flock your business and do not be tempted by the wonders being wrought in Africa and the east.

"Think only of Britain and your own important task. Immediate success is not our ambition, the will of the Lord is our only concern.

"Deep foundations mean a large building, and deep stones are hidden. Do your work well with our little flock, and concentrate on giving them deep learning and piety so that they in turn can support the work of others.

"It is not for you to be a witness with great preaching and outwardly visible. Yours is the hidden work of dedication to our future priests and servers of the Lord. Train them well, God will be with you. He will be the witness of your doings and will bless you and take you into his arms for eternity. I have seen his love with my own eyes and know it to be true."

After parting from them at the jetty Joseph climbed the little cliff to watch their boat sail. He kept his eyes on the little figures on the deck and thought he saw his son wave.

The boat sailed into the gray sea until it was lost to sight where the dark clouds met the horizon. Sky and sea merged into a mist.

While he watched them disappear, he felt as though his wife was leaning her head and shoulder against his chest. He seemed to feel his arm resting on her shoulder, just as he used to do when they were saying farewells to her parents or visiting brothers and sisters. Then she used to lean against him for support and consolation, as they said their farewells on the porch of their house.

When the ship merged into the mist, Joseph went to the altar to pray. The little light glowed in the dark room, Joseph knelt first, and then after a few minutes sat before the Holy of Holies, the little shrine covered with a miniature veil copied from the veil of the Temple in Jerusalem.

As he prayed, for an instant his person felt as though it were expanding from his body, reaching back in time till it almost touched the gates of the Garden of Eden; and he heard the shofars blowing, and yet the sound was muffled by time until they sounded to his ears like the ringing of a deep sea bell.

Frozen in an instant, his being seemed to sweep past the little boat tossing in the channel; it crossed the Mediterranean to swirl around Jerusalem. And all this was accompanied by an indescribable peace and contentment. Past and present and all distance seemed frozen in one glorious stillness.

"Oh Lord, is this the delight of the Garden of Eden, which Adam threw away by eating the apple of self-love?"

The moment faded, and Joseph was back to himself.

CHAPTER 27

## ⚘ The Kitchen

Meanwhile Eleanor's heart was being tossed in the surging
cross tides of different emotions.

First she was petrified about Joseph's reaction to David's
leaving. How would he take the pain of separation?

Her thoughts turned to David. She had come to love the boy
deeply, like a fussy aunt.

She loved the refinement of his ways, his care of the little
details of courtesy, that gentle wit, his steadfastness, his quiet
toughness in putting up with discomfort, and always the smiling
good humor.

Life would be dull without him, and the people would
miss him.

Anxiety also weighed heavily on her heart for the safety of
the little band as they journeyed to Greece—thinking of the dangers and temptations they would meet in a land of such sophistication and pagan culture. Would they be dazzled by its apparent
glamour and abandon the cross of Christ?

Eleanor hurried to prepare Joseph's favorite dish for supper and
was just about ready when Joseph emerged from the altar room.

He sat down. looked at Eleanor and spoke. "Eleanor, for the
children of God there is no such thing as time or distance; these

things are linked to mortality and we must seek the things that do not pass away. We must seek the omnipresence of God; through him we are all united past, present, and future."

Eleanor didn't understand what he meant; but he looked convinced, and so she was contented and nodded.

Joseph looked down and suddenly noticed her hands, swollen at the joints and red. He held them in his own hands, cupping them between his and then he prayed: "Lord, I have never asked for physical miracles, being content with thy Holy Will. May I make an exception just this once? Please keep these hands and joints supple, serving thee, until the moment of her death on earth."

At that instant the pain left her hands, back, knees, and ankles; she suddenly realized how much her growing ailment had been contributing to her unease.

She never mentioned this incident to anyone until long after Joseph's death.

A knock on the door; then it was opened and, in the doorway, the head of Mulfra appeared. It was rather like the head of a fox looking into a chicken hut.

He brought in a large basket, and out came sealed jars bearing his different ferments. Mulfra prided himself on his ability to make wine out of different fruits and herbs, sweetened with honey. Dried meats and fish and salt cheese, followed with butter and hardened bread. Next came his flute.

Here was Mulfra, the bard, about to entertain and give solace to his friends.

The singing, music, and conversation lasted until the early hours. They both escorted Eleanor home, and Mulfra returned to finish the evening asleep on the cushions by the fire in Joseph's home.

# CHAPTER 28

## ✣ Letters

The burden of work became heavy for all of them as the remaining teachers struggled to make up for the loss. It fell particularly hard on Demas as he continued to administer the Sacraments. Many nights were sleepless as he consoled the dying or walked through the night to celebrate the Eucharist as promised to his flock in some of the more outlying districts.

Joseph arranged for transport to bring the flock to the shepherd as much as possible, rather than sending the shepherd out to his sheep, and there were long lines as people confessed their sins to Demas one by one and he sent each one away with his blessing. His soldier constitution stood him in good stead, but he began to tire and everyone feared for his health.

Prayers were said for a solution, and the miracle happened.

A Roman builder, brought over for the new constructions, had a son, Antonius, who was a new priest converted in Rome and sent by the brethren when they heard of his father's contract in Britain.

Even in Rome they had heard of the British community. Antonius was closely related to the prominent patrician Glabrio family. And he was to be of considerable help.

He obtained Roman citizenship for Joseph, Eleanor, and the families of Morvah and Mulfra.

The Roman authorities were eager to establish alliances and to obtain loyal citizens among the British in order to strengthen their administrative hold over the country.

Antonius submitted himself readily to the intensive British language course, bringing some of his Roman administrators and government officials, who paid useful cash. Some of these converted to the Way, but he failed with his own father.

Maybe he tried too hard.

But his father was tolerant and allowed his arm to be twisted for loans of equipment and workmen when needed.

And his father's men taught some of the British how to work stone and hired them for Roman projects.

Eleanor received a letter. It had been written by a scribe on behalf of her father.

*"Most beloved, illustrious, and much loved daughter; the finest gift that your loving mother ever gave to me and source of much of my happiness and consolation. I am not much longer to remain on this earth, and by the time this letter reaches you I probably shall have departed to join my heavenly Father and my beloved wife, who I am sure is waiting for me with him.*

*"Jesus is merciful and grants our requests. . . . I leave with joy and hope in my heart. . . . The days, when my existence was filled with quiet desperation, are long gone. . . . The small hopes of each day, our petty successes, and the quiet despair when our puny plans go badly have been filled and made joyous by the over all hope of life itself . . .*

*"Through the life of Jesus, my life has been given new meaning, and the precarious hold on life, once held because I lacked only a specific reason for dying, has been filled with a new fire. . . . The fear in the old creed has died out; and my limitations, which lay sickeningly on my heart, making my illusions of mastery merely a mockery, have been laid like some slaughtered lamb at the feet of my Heavenly Master . . .*

*"In shedding false hope, I have gained new hope, because I am
no longer ignorant of life's meaning. I await you eagerly in Heaven,
where I shall be able to recompense you for any wrong I have done to
you. Forgive me and love me always . . .*

   *"Till we meet again . . .*

                                        *"Your ever loving father,*
                                        *"Dauwid."*

Eleanor left immediately for the land of the Chun. When she
arrived he was already in a coma, and he died soon afterwards in
her arms.

Soon after the funeral, she left the election of the new king to
the elders, laying down only one command, that the successor be
a worthy Christian, who among the Christian princes should
have a reputation for sound government.

She returned to Fal before the election.

David's letters had already arrived, one for Joseph and one
for Eleanor.

Hers was a thank-you letter with news of events during his
travels and the journey subsequent to leaving the group at Corinth.

David had installed them in the training school and then left
immediately for Ephesus to find his mother and take the letter
sent by Joseph.

David had written the letters from Ephesus.

*"Dearest Father,*

*"It is with deep sorrow and with many prayers and supplications
that I have to announce that beloved Mama has passed from this life
to the glorious Kingdom of Heaven where she awaits us.*

   *"She had died some time before my arrival, and I calculate that
it was at or a little time before our departure from Britain.*

   *"Mary tended to her last days, and her death was filled with
sweetness and consolation. Neither Ruth nor Karen was able to
attend the funeral; the message reached them too late and Ruth was
not able to afford the trip. The work is poor and hard and they have
been unable to win the support of influential families in the region.*

"*Karen has sent a message that she is coming to join me for a short while, taking a fast boat down the Nile. I shall give her a copy of the letter from you. I have already sent your letter to Ruth, along with some of your money by one of the priests who travels to that region. If you can replace this gift by sending money to Corinth, I too shall be most grateful.*

"*Karen has promised help also and is persuading the Egyptians to adopt the region as a recipient for help and assistance. We had not been aware of Ruth's difficulties since she had never complained or asked for help. The slaves are cruelly treated there and there are many converts among them. Their prayers and personal sacrifice, offered from the crucible of their sufferings to our Father God for us will amply recompense us for our material gifts.*

"*Their steadfastness in faith and endurance is wonderful; many beautiful hymns to the Passion of Christ have been composed by them, some of them written to popular tunes from the plays of the Greek dramatists. Among the slaves are Jews of great learning. They are teaching the Christians the language of the scriptures; although they will not convert, they are impressed by the simplicity and piety of their slave compatriots and are willing to teach them. They are united in suffering together and offering it to the Lord.*

"*Some slaves have escaped and live their Christian lives in the desert. Some are willing to come to Britain so that their prayers may help our region. Their life in the desert is very austere. I am arranging for their travel. They will carry letters from my own hand in British, so that no impostors can deceive you. The bearer of this letter is one of them. Greet him with the kiss of the saints and supply his needs. More of his companions will follow later. They prefer to live remote from this world.*

"*Once established, they will be self-sufficient. I cannot give you news about Mary since it might jeopardize her safety. John is on Patmos. Send many more prospective priests and dedicated women to Corinth. I remember your wise counsel. The things you spoke about are already happening. I have assumed British identity, as it gives me greater safety.*

"*Jerusalem is no more. The Romans have destroyed it.*

"*Nothing remains of the Temple, and everyone is stunned into grief and silence. The revolt and subsequent siege was bloody and terrible, a living hell on earth. The city was ringed with crosses and the price of slaves has plummeted because so many, captured after the siege, have been sold into slavery. The arenas are filled with the cries of captured slaves, and the whole community is filled with grief and lamentation.*

"*I have managed to get hold of some earth from the site of the Temple in Jerusalem. It is carried by the bearer of this letter. It is all that is left . . . just bare earth and obtained at great personal risk.*

"*Jews are not allowed in Israel and have been scattered around the empire. The rift between the Judaizing party and the Greek Christians has been healed in the calamity. The whole community offers comfort to each other.*

"*Mary (I hope I am quoting her correctly) has said that all these things are meant to pass. Satan as part of his punishment on Earth is tied to matter.*

"*The old Temple of wood and stone has passed away and the new Temple must now reside in Spirit in the hearts of those who love her Son.*

"*The fabric of this new Temple must be our virtues, put in place by our efforts, aided by grace. It is here that the Holy Spirit will reside.*

"*A new heart I will give you, and a new spirit I will put within you; and I will take out of your flesh the heart of stone and give you a heart of flesh. And I will put my spirit within and cause you to walk in my statutes and be careful to observe my ordinances*"*(Ezekiel 36:26–27).*

"*The physical presence of her Beloved Son will grace every Temple built to his honor where the Eucharist is celebrated.*

"*There shall not be just one Temple in the future, but many, on mountain and in valley, in town and in the countryside and in every nation*—another Angel came forward to meet him. He said to him 'Run and tell that young man this':

"*Jerusalem is to remain unwalled because of the great number of men and cattle there will be in her. 'But I*—it is the Lord who speaks—'I will be a wall of fire for her all round her. I will be her glory in the midst of her.'

" 'Sing and rejoice, O daughter of Zion, for lo I come and I will dwell in the midst of you, says the Lord. And many nations will join themselves to the Lord in that day, and shall be my people' (Zechariah 2:3–5, 10–11)."

"She has been a great comfort to us in these troubled times.

"I shall return to Corinth, as soon as my work is finished here. I shall write to you from there. Everyone sends greetings. Ruth and Karen will write separately once we have established channels of communication. Farewell for the present.

"Your letter has been read out and copies made for the joy and consolation of us all.

"I have mounted the crucifix you made for Mama on a plaque of finest marble and surrounding it, the gold chain in the shape of the Star of David. It rests on the altar for every celebration of the Eucharist.

> Your loving son,
> David."

# CHAPTER 29

## ⚜ Rebecca's Odyssey

When Joseph had left for work, Rebecca had questioned the servants about the supposed appearance of Jesus to them.

She questioned them separately and they all recounted the same story about his appearing to them, while they were preparing the evening meal. He had walked among them taking their hands and kissing them each and everyone of them. He thanked them personally for preparing his body for burial.

They had all recognized him as the Master and had seen the scars on his hands and feet, just as they had washed them in preparation for burial. He asked them to be faithful to him, since a great deal depended on their loyalty.

Rebecca was mystified by the consistency of each of their stories. And she was still pondering the mystery when guards arrived and she and her family were arrested.

As she was being escorted out of her house, she saw Azim. She looked away from him to another servant and shouted out in Hebrew: "Azim, they are arresting us. Look for Joseph and tell him. Tell him to be careful."

The guards seized the servant, giving time for Azim to make his escape. By the time they had questioned the other servant,

Azim had left. Rebecca, Ruth and Karen were kept together in the Roman barracks. The guards had not included David, who had been with the maids.

It had been the maid holding David who had run to Mary. Mary wasted no time, but went immediately to Pilate's palace. The maid of Pilate's wife came to her gatherings, and she admitted Mary to see Pilate's wife.

Whatever Mary said to her remained private but the effect was that Pilate was immediately contacted and that he issued an order of release which was dispatched then and there to the soldiers' quarters.

Rebecca and her daughters returned to an empty house. Sensing imminent danger Rebecca rushed to Reuben, who wasted no time in contacting Callistus, having made enquiries about the arrest and about who had issued the order.

Callistus was still rubbing his neck when Reuben called on him, armed with scrolls tucked under his arm. The scrolls contained details of the 'private activities' of Callistus. They held a discussion for over an hour while Reuben cleverly gleaned from a shaken Callistus the whole plot.

After the meeting Reuben took his time; the immediate danger was over. Callistus had agreed that for him to ally himself with Reuben was the safest option as far as his security was concerned.

Caiphas was a much trickier customer. Joseph had always been too much of an idealist in his dealings with Caiphas. Cold naked fear was the only thing Caiphas appreciated, and Reuben needed time to think how he could deliver that to him. Two days later Reuben arranged to meet Caiphas. He stressed that for Caiphas' own sake their meeting should be private.

Caiphas complied. He was already deeply concerned about the absence of Callistus. Speed and decisive action had always been the essence of his strategy: use the powerful by planting the story first and generating the reaction before the enemy has time to recover his forces and counterattack.

The confiscation of property had failed to materialize, and he wanted to avoid showing complicity in the scheme by making enquiries. The populace would not appreciate his methods of subtle diplomacy and power politics: his plans might look like betrayal of a Jew to a Roman for personal gain.

"Hello Caiphas, I am pleased to see you. I haven't seen you for a long time. You know me: don't have much time for meeting people. Too much time taken up with administration, figures, accounts, buying and selling, documents, documents. It never ends. I am very grateful for your being so kind as to spare me a little of your time."

The style made Caiphas even more nervous. Reuben didn't seem in a hurry.

"Well, Reuben, if you asked to see me then I knew it must be important. I know we are both busy so I shall appreciate your getting down to business."

"Thank you, Caiphas. I have been thinking about how to introduce these matters politely.

"Clever move you made to tell the Assyrian mercenaries that Jesus was the one who had been organizing the assassination of their soldiers, using the Sicarii. Along with the bribe they did a very good job with the flogging. Pity it wasn't true, because we both know who is behind that don't we?"

Reuben passed a document to Caiphas.

"How contact is made, by whom, and through what intermediaries. I am sure these people will reveal all, under the refinements of Roman torture.

"Now the one thing the Romans can't stand is double dealing, because they themselves do it all the time and they don't like rivals.

"For you, Caiphas, it will be a one-way trip to Rome as Rome's special guest. Maybe even an opportunity for a solitary performance in an arena."

"You wouldn't dare, Reuben!"

"Wouldn't dare? It has nothing to do with me. I have no control over my friend Callistus."

"Your friend Callistus?" Caiphas went a deathly white.

"Oh yes. He has written a full account of your attempts at stealing."

"Written?"

"Yes, written."

Reuben tossed a copy of the account into Caiphas' lap and he read through it quickly.

"Yes, it is unusual for a top administrator to commit himself to writing like that. Even he must have been appalled by your treachery. Now, Caiphas, I am willing to forget the attempts at harm you have made on my family. After all we are both Jews, and dealing with foreigners is always a nasty business. Agreed?"

"Agreed."

"Now in return for my help with Callistus I want no more trouble, and I want no more persecution of the followers of Christ. I would take it amiss if you were to bear grudges like that. Grudges aren't good in a man of religion. And I wouldn't want to see a man of such distinction ending up in Rome. You are needed here."

Reuben patted Caiphas on the knee.

"Agreed?"

"Agreed."

Reuben said nothing else, gathered up the documents, and left.

Later, Azim returned and found the situation better than expected. In creeping around the house he had heard Rebecca's voice, then Ruth and Karen. He waited until dawn, then crept around to Assab in the stable apartments and sent him out to find out what was happening. Only later in the day did he emerge from hiding to give his account of the story.

The death sentence against Joseph was still held by Callistus as a bargaining counter against Reuben, and he still held Joseph to blame for the attempt on his life. No bribe would make him change his mind, and the more they tried the more he realized that this was the one thing of value that he held against them. Joseph's death sentence was the guarantee for his own safety. Reuben knew too much about him for his comfort and security.

Reuben and the Apostles decided that with the unpredictability of the situation in Jerusalem, there could be a sudden reversal of fortune. It would be better for Rebecca and the family to secretly move a safe distance from Jerusalem.

Rebecca was now in a constant state of nerves at the narrowness of her escape from death, and confidence in the security of her family needed to be restored. Everyone needed rest and tranquillity.

Part of Rebecca's nervousness was the fear that Joseph would return. An attempt on the life of a Roman official warranted special punishment. Spies were everywhere, and Joseph would almost certainly be betrayed. The type of death that Joseph would face was too horrible to contemplate.

Mary advised Rebecca to let Joseph remain in the mission that the Lord had entrusted to him. Though stressing that they were free, she indicated that Joseph had been chosen as a special object of her Son's care and attention.

Rebecca asked Azim to leave a message at Marsalla that the family had suddenly disappeared and that the Roman authorities were looking for Joseph. Rebecca resigned herself to seeing her husband no more.

Reuben supervised the move to the north. Everybody traveled under assumed names, individually. He also arranged for the transfer of funds for the upkeep of the family and for the needs of the work being done there, as Joseph would have wished.

Azim acted as courier.

Rebecca devoted all of her energies to the education of the children, especially of the baby David. They had only a few servants because of their straitened circumstances and because the work of the Christian community made demands on their finances. Luxuries were kept to a minimum, usually to give joy to her children on special occasions. Rebecca began to do much of the housework herself, and this along with the charitable works of the community made her life busy.

The girls were already old enough to help with household chores, but Mary encouraged Rebecca to give them an education beyond what was customary for women of the region. Mary stressed that study, serious concentrated study, opened the soul to prayer. Later, prayer and study would become handmaids to one another; both would help one to seek closer union with her Son. And so, besides their household work both Ruth and Karen studied.

Despite the difficulty, Rebecca also took up the role of student. Her chief concern was the education of David. She now no longer had Joseph to help her.

Jesus' mother gave many classes on the upbringing of children. Without giving direct instructions to parents, she described the development of her own Son. She described how different qualities became manifest at different ages, as a guide for the growth in virtue of their own children. She gave the story of her own Son's childhood as an example for them to imitate in the development of their children. The parents would discuss among themselves the qualities they wanted to see develop at different ages.

Mary stressed and gave examples of the good humor, joy, and wit of her Son. She stressed the importance of joy and optimism. She also mentioned the importance of teaching politeness and good manners to little children, since this was the way eventually they would learn to live and be concerned for the needs of others, gradually learning to forget themselves and also learning to put God first, others second, and themselves last.

David was a joy to Rebecca.

It's easy for a mother to love a son: the odd things they keep in their pockets, their boyish ways, the enthusiasm they have for adventure, competitions which seem to occupy all of their attention so they can hardly be persuaded to think about anything else. The emotional dependency they have as children on their mothers, makes them loveable, even though at times they try to hide it as unmanly.

David was a naturally friendly boy, and Rebecca took great care in the selection of his friends. Sometimes she would be quite strict with him, when he wanted to go off with companions whom Rebecca did not approve of.

He would sometimes sulk over his mother's apparently unreasonable behavior.

On one occasion Mary came to speak to him when he was in one of his moods. She laid down a simple guide for him about the selection of friends. A good friend is someone of great value and must not be treated lightly. "A friend can take you to heaven or to hell," was the gist of Mary's remarks. This was all that Rebecca could glean from David afterwards.

David took after his father in intelligence and was encouraged by everyone to study hard. He chose medicine for his career but did not abandon his Greek, Roman, and Hebrew learning. While working as a doctor he indicated to his mother that he thought he should be a priest. His ordination came rather quickly, since he had spent a lifetime in study.

Rebecca experienced three spiritual funerals, first when Ruth told her that she felt called to work among the Parthians. Ruth had Joseph's intelligence and a little of his temperament and Rebecca could discuss important issues with her. She appreciated her thoughtful advice.

Rebecca seemed to lose a confidante as well as a daughter when she left, walking along the road towards Parthia with the other Christian women who were going there. A little wave just before she passed out of sight was the last Rebecca would ever see of her.

Later she again felt bereaved with the departure of Karen to Egypt.

Karen was a joy and would often tease her mother and amuse her with her gushing enthusiasms. Karen gave a tearful smile, as she vigorously waved her goodbye. It was a long time before she came back on a business visit, and her joy and laughter rippled round the house once more. David was beside himself with joy on that occasion.

Rebecca's heart lay bleeding for several days after her departure, and David entered into a depressed hope that she would return again soon.

The experience of grief was almost as intense as at a funeral; but the "corpse" was living, breathing, smiling and waving. Rebecca sympathized with the parents of dead children. She could hardly bear her grief, and her children were still alive.

The pain of David's departure was a dull and heavy anguish. Mary had asked David if he would like to go to seek his father. News had reached Rome that there was a Christian community in southwest Britain. His father was likely to be there.

David said yes.

Rebecca's final support and consolation was removed when David told her of his intention. She tried to hide her pain since she did not want to deter him from his mission.

She had gradually learned to live without Joseph and had done the best she could for the children in his absence. David's declaration of his intention reopened old wounds and she longed for Joseph's company.

She longed to go with David, but her age and failing health would not allow her to. She had resisted all temptations to make contact with her husband. It would have been the same as issuing a death sentence, especially when Britain came under Roman influence and jurisdiction.

Joseph might also be dead, and the whole journey would be in vain. She could only be a burden for David. Mary also wanted her to look after some of the younger women.

Over the following days she worked on a letter for Joseph hoping that it would find him alive and well. She also instructed David not to send word back by somebody else that Joseph was alive. He could only do that in person by telling her himself.

Joseph was not to come to her. Spies abounded, and hatred for Jews in the area was increasing due to the troubles in Israel.

Rebecca went with him to the ship having carefully packed provisions for the journey and some heavier clothing because she knew that the weather was colder in the North. Having entrusted her son with the letter and present for her husband, and given him a long farewell embrace, she sat on boxes by the quayside as the ship slowly made headway. Sitting down made things a little more bearable. She feared that if stood she might faint, and cause David great distress.

"Oh, Jesus, you seem to have sent all my little ones to the ends of the earth. Your work must be important for you not to allow us to cling to earthly consolation."

Rebecca prayed as the ship moved out of sight. She waited an hour by the quayside, staring at the water and at the light dancing on the waves until she had regained her composure.

She was not to see David again.

Mary came to her to comfort her, and she stressed how important the work was which had been entrusted to her family.

Because Joseph had been so brave and had been such a consolation to her when he had buried her Son in his own grave, she had made him and Britain the special object of her love and affection. Great things depended on their faithfulness.

Rebecca threw herself into the work of the Christian community; and all her thoughts, words, and actions were offered as prayer for the work of her husband, daughters, and son. She often would imagine their work in those far-off lands and what life would be like there. She tried to read about life in those places and was eager when letters arrived, giving news about activities of the different Christian communities around the world.

She had many friends, and these were a great consolation. They loved her very much and she loved them.

Years passed, and Rebecca never heard from David. She hoped and prayed he was still alive and would be able one day to come and visit her.

She waited in vain.

Rioting against Jews had broken out in the town with news of the revolt taking place in Israel. There had been massacres of Jews.

Rebecca bolted the doors of her house; but the mob had been directed there by a disaffected Christian, and they began to break down the door. The terror of the immanent entry of the mob was too much for Rebecca's heart.

When the mob finally broke through the door, they found only a corpse on the floor.

# CHAPTER 30

## ✤ Reuben's Story

Reuben's life in Jerusalem was not easy. He kept out of politics as far as he could but hatreds die hard and he maintained his network of informants, hoping to avoid any unpleasant surprises. The serving maid of Caiphas served him well. He had always been kind to her family and was now even more solicitous, making sure the help was discrete and haphazard so that it could not be traced back to him.

Years passed, and Reuben watched the family grow up.

He never remarried after his wife died but became the favorite uncle.

His relaxation was to take time off to visit Rebecca's family and check the education of the children. He spent the odd moments of his leisure time in Jerusalem planning presents and surprises for them. He really enjoyed the squeals of delight when his entourage appeared outside their house.

He attended some of the religious activities of the Christians along with Mary and other pious folk and attended the baptism of Rebecca and her children. Mary spent much of her time traveling from one group of women to another and rarely rested long in any one place. Her work was constant and strenuous.

Ruth was eventually sent by Mary to the Parthians.

Azim had gone earlier with the men-folk.

Karen similarly went to Egypt, following work done by the disciples, eventually ending in Upper Egypt.

Rebecca had not adapted well to single life, since she didn't have a strong temperament. Her worry about Joseph had brought on a heart condition, and her ankles would sometimes swell. She had to sleep propped up on cushions to help her breathing.

Reuben viewed events in Jerusalem with growing disquiet. He hired extra guards to protect his properties in the face of increasing lawlessness. Roman reprisals were getting more and more brutal, and this brutality inflamed the people. The zealots were working feverishly inciting reprisals that were followed by counter-reprisals. Everybody began to fear for the worst. Feelings were running high on all sides. The normal reaction of the soldiers was brutality. Fear ruled everywhere; even walking on the street was hazardous since a person might be caught up in a sudden and random round up of hostages.

The revolt started with an attack on the barracks by an enraged mob, this time supported by armed men trained in secret in the countryside and smuggled into Jerusalem.

Callistus had gone to leave food at the leper colony, and this act of charity had saved his life. The lepers brought him into their camp, and no one betrayed him. In fact nobody chose to come near them during the whole of the fighting and tumult in the city. He had taken off his Roman finery and donned the mantle of a leper, a courageous act that had not been part of his military training. His disguise saved his life, but it also prevented his reaching Cestius when he attempted to retake the city. He would have been killed. He could not find a way of getting to him as a leper, who could not jostle his way through the crowd. His failure to join with Cestius saved him from the disastrous retreat of the Roman army to Antipatris.

Callistus had come without money. He was not in the habit of carrying money. He was already hungry and had stopped off at the colony on his way back to his quarters to eat. Now he waited all afternoon in the heat while he tried to figure out what to do. He put two pebbles in his mouth to hide his Roman accent when he spoke Aramaic, and set out to beg. Roman bodies were lying everywhere, slaughtered, men, women, children, and an occasional Roman soldier caught unawares.

He saw the dead bodies of his own wife and children. Seeing their dead bodies was almost a relief. He had felt ill with worry at what might have happened to them and whether they had become the sport of a vicious crowd, but their death had been swift. He sought psychological refuge in military-style routine. He crushed his emotions.

Fighting was still going on at the barracks, but there was no food and little water. The Romans' resistance would not last long; lack of sleep would defeat them even before hunger and thirst.

Callistus tried to beg, but nobody took any notice. He tried all afternoon and evening but all to no avail. He returned to the leper colony and almost felt like crying, but there was still enough Roman pride to prevent it. He steeled himself by refusing to think of the past or future.

"You still haven't mastered the art of begging—where to go, how to ask. It's a hard business, but praying to God for our daily bread is the most natural of our tasks."

The man sat on the ground beside Callistus, split his own meager rations and gave a portion to Callistus. Callistus noticed that he had received the more generous portion.

"How long have you been a leper?" asked Callistus.

"I am not a leper, but was asked by the brethren to work with them. I practiced medicine, and my name is Stephas. I am a disciple of Jesus."

"I have met Jesus-worshippers before." Callistus cheered up as food entered his stomach, and he felt a wave of affection for his new friend. "Listen, my friend, a word in your ear. Follow my advice. Give honor and cult to the Roman gods, Jupiter, Zeus to the Greeks, and the like. I figure it this way:

"There is continual warfare going on in the heavens, unseen by us, but it reflects conflict here below. Sometimes some gods are in the ascendancy and at other times others. The Roman gods are mighty. So give honor and worship to them. The Jews don't realize what they have let themselves in for. They have never seen Roman legions angry at atrocities committed against their own kind. It's going to be a terrible, terrible spectacle. Jupiter and Mars will destroy the God of Israel. If death is not possible for the gods, then the God of Israel will be reduced to passing mention in the history books."

"When the Roman army returns to restore Roman order to Israel I shall not forget your kindness, my friend. I hope that you witness a Roman army in full battle; the gods shall see the might of Jupiter and Mars and their exceeding anger."

"These battles are for fools and drunks." Stephas held Callistus in his gaze as he spoke. "Do you know what the real battle is?

"It is a battle of personal combat against an enemy stronger and cleverer than we humans. His presence is terrible to behold. With his trident he tries to hook off our shield and cuirass. He stabs at our wrist to loose the hold on our sword. We fight him with sword, shield, and helmet, jumping like a rabbit to miss the sweep of his snare net, our sweat and tears dripping from our face onto the sand. It is a combat to the death without respite. This is the real battle that men are called to fight daily."

"You are telling me a child's story," smiled Callistus.

"In one sense, yes, in another, no. The fight we have daily is the fight against our enemy, the devil, a fallen angel of great intelligence. He revolted against our God, Yahweh, and was defeated by an archangel called Michael. Lucifer, this fallen angel, was cast into hell, a place of terrible fire and suffering, along with all other wicked spirits, but he was granted time to roam the Earth seeking earthlings whom he desires to entice into hell. Humans were created secondarily by God to take the place of those angels who had revolted. The devil has countless tricks to tempt man into vice. He tries to snare us into the net of evil, violence, hatred, rancor, pride, covetousness, lust. He stabs at us with the trident of lies and false promises."

"Doesn't it hurt and depress lepers to tell them these things about combat, since some have rotting limbs?" asked Callistus.

"No," answered Stephas. "They understand that this combat takes place inside the soul of each and every one of us; and those with sound limbs and healthy bodies are often disadvantaged because in their contentment they can fall more easily into the traps of the devil. Lepers fight harder in spiritual combat than the healthy.

"Christ, by his death on the cross, promised us victory if we follow his directions. In some mysterious way, beyond our understanding, God has made suffering and death into instruments for the salvation of mankind. We have to accept that with our faith, not our understanding.

"We have to wear the breastplate of justice, the helmet of salvation, and the sword of the spirit, God's word: with these we fight the evils of Satan. Yet the worst enemy we have is ourselves. What are we good for if our souls are weakened by debauchery and sensuous living? How can we be fit for combat? We have to live the life and discipline of an athlete so that our soul is fit and healthy. We have to wash and clean our soul from all contamination, by confessing our sins to God, so that it is free from corruption and we must oil our spiritual muscles with charity so that they are smooth and supple and slippery to the enemy.

"The battles of great armies happen when men become mad, mad for power, lusting for possession without effort, drunk with hatred, and debauched by love of pleasure.

"The battles of armies are punishments allowed by God, so that mankind in misery will turn away from false pleasures, sloth, and pride and turn again to things of the spirit. To the battle for purity of soul. That is the real battle. It is a battle for love of God, love of others, and lastly love of self.

"It is the battle for right order within ourselves, within the kingdom of one's own soul, which will reflect itself, in consequence, in peace and order in the state. The good of the state is the sum of the good of its citizens, as Plato said. When you said my description of mortal combat was a story, you were partly right, but yet in another sense this combat is in deadly earnest. Our battle is a spiritual one, which takes place in the depths of our souls. This is the real battle which concerns us."

Callistus spent his days with Stephas, tending the sores of lepers, while Stephas talked to him. He went out to beg like the others.

He got a kind of satisfaction from his work. He did not have to look over his shoulder constantly at the ambitious, anxious for promotion. Political plots and temporary alliances all seemed like a past dream.

Life had become simple.

He wandered through areas near, and sometimes inside, Jerusalem, begging and watching the preparations for the defense of the city. He sometimes carefully disguised himself, not as a leper, as these were not allowed in the city, but as an ordinary beggar and thus entered the city. He tried to keep clear of the factional fighting and the blood-letting. He made note of the Jews' defensive positions and strong points, because such information could be useful later for the Roman Army. He made drawings back at the colony from his furtive sketches and hid them.

Food became difficult to get, especially after the burning of the granaries in the city by the rival Jewish factions. He became very, very hungry.

Callistus's hunger made him more bold. He reached out to a wealthy looking man entering the city, ringing his bell as he begged. The man bent down picked up a rock, and threw it at him with all his might. It hit him on the shoulder and knocked him to the ground. Callistus lay there, not daring to get up.

"Get away from me, leper. You are too bold; keep your distance."

A hand took his arm, and Callistus looked up and saw Reuben.

Reuben turned to the stone thrower and said, "Let him alone. Enough misfortune has fallen on this man, there is no reason for you to make it worse." Callistus drew his head cloth closer across his face so that Reuben would not recognize him.

"Take this. It is a key to that house with the white tower," said Reuben. "I am choosing to stay in the city, and if you don't take it the Romans soon will when they arrive. Tell the other lepers to move in with you. In the cellar there is a new brick wall. Knock it down and there you will find food hidden behind it. If you go sparingly. It should last you until the final resolution of this conflict. I fear for this city. Madmen are now in charge."

"You are a wonderful man," lisped Callistus, "to care for people who are so unclean."

"My friend," Reuben raised his voice slightly, "some people look clean on the outside, but their souls are filth and corruption; and some people look defiled on the outside, but inside is harmony and sweetness. I am one of the former, my friend. So as a Jew, pray for me."

Reuben tossed the key to Callistus and hurried on his way to the city.

A triumphant Callistus entered the leper colony holding the key, the most successful beggar of them all, and briefly enjoyed the cheers of his compatriots. They soon were drifting in ones and twos to their new dwelling. Signs were made indicating that it was a leper colony, an effective way to keep out looters.

Tension mounted as news came of the approaching army and of the defeats of Jews in other parts of the country by Vespasian. Callistus in various disguises listened to the gossip about the internal dissensions in the city. He heard about the death of Ananus, the high priest, and the terrible slaughter among the people of the city by the Zealots and the Idumeans. He saw the fear in the people from the night-time arrests and the torture of the leading nobility, the show trials organized by the Zealots

using puppet judges to give some semblance of legality. The
Zealots profaned the Temple and ridiculed the ceremonies of the
priests, calling them tricks of jugglers to fool the people. Some of
them were lewd in their behavior.

The Romans had not shown such disrespect.

He saw the bodies of the dead piled high by the roads—
people killed for trying to escape the city. The Zealots refused
them burial. The fearful who had fled to the city at first were now
held there by that same fear.

Hatred spread through the streets like a flood, back and forth,
lapping the doorways of the houses as people were dragged out
for interrogation. It burst out of the city gates into the nearby villages with the plundering parties, whose excuse was the gathering
of provisions for the defense of the city, but whose real motive
was often robbery. The promise of a Jewish paradise on earth
became like a carrion crow, hopping over the congealing and
drying blood, flitting between the rotting corpses and settling
with ruffled feathers into the crags of men's hearts.

It became a slogan which nobody believed.

Jerusalem had become a bleak and cavernous tomb.

Callistus was almost disappointed when he heard the distant
rumble and creaking of a moving army. He thought the Jews
themselves were doing a better job of destroying the city than
the Romans ever could. They had already killed many of their
best fighting troops and the noblest and most courageous of
their kindred.

Callistus, back at the colony, donned his Roman clothing,
carefully cleaned and polished his uniform, and then put over it
the mantle of leper. He said goodbye to his lepers, promising that
he would not forget them.

He stood by the roadside and waited until the Jewish skir-
mishers retreated past him. In the no-man's-land between the
retreating Jews and the advancing Romans he hid behind some
rocks, took off his mantle and then stood in the road, sword in his
hand, with the sun glinting on his armor.

The sound of horses and the crunch of feet drew nearer. The dust obscured the detail, and at first he couldn't see the standards of the legions. Later he made out the V, the X, and the XII. The latter had been in the retreat with Cestius. Callistus waited in the middle of the road; as they came within sight of him he raised his sword as an indication for the first column to halt.

"Hail Caesar!" Callistus shouted out the greeting as early as he could so that he would not attract the javelin of an over-zealous skirmisher. He strode forward as the first cohort came up to him, took a wax tablet out of the hand of a scribe accompanying the main party, punched his signet ring into it, and told the man to give it to Titus, son of Vespasian, having asked him the name of the commander. He had known Titus, since Vespasian and he had trained together in Rome. Titus had often watched them in mock combat.

"I am not yet Caesar. Aren't you Callistus? I recognize you from Military School in Rome.

"Yes, sir."

"What are you doing here?"

"Defending the empire of Rome."

Laughter rippled through the horsemen around Titus.

"Where are your men?"

"Dead."

"I was envious of your fighting prowess in training. How did you survive?"

"As you know, Sir, I can use the sword equally well in either hand. And so I rested one arm while I used the other."

Another peal of laughter followed from the men.

"Well, Callistus, you must be short on sleep if you have been fighting Jews since the revolt."

"It's not so much the sleep, sir, but I would like to go to the toilet."

Amidst the loud guffaws, Titus indicated that he wanted to see Callistus in his tent as soon as they had set camp.

Callistus took the scouts to a good site, easily defensible, with a good view of the city and its approaches. The helmets of the

Jewish defenders glistened reddish in the sun, like pin-points of light glistening from the battlements.

Callistus watched the men marching past and then the ox carts with equipment and provisions, massive in size and number. The thrill of military pride ran through his veins. Later he watched the approach of the siege engines, slave and beast sweating and suffering with the exertion and encouraged by the lash.

Callistus was given a luxurious tent close to Titus.

The temporary defenses of the Roman camp and the arrangement and protection of the equipment took a few days. Water supplies were secured for the camp.

As the camp began to settle down into routine, Callistus received a summons to attend a council meeting with the senior officers. Callistus had not been idle in the intervening days. He had been drawing up his plans of the city and its defenses, and estimates of the size of the army opposing them in the city. Callistus took the scrolls with him in a large linen satchel.

Callistus sat to the rear of the group around Titus and listened to the reports from various sections of the army about their state of preparedness. There had been skirmishes already, some involving Titus, in the gardens north of the city.

Titus then asked his senior commanders for their suggestions about how the attack should proceed. All of them were for immediate attack before the defenders could become organized and experienced in co-ordinating their defense of the city.

"What do you think, Callistus?" Titus suddenly remembered Callistus was present amongst them.

Callistus stood up and all eyes turned to him. They were still mystified as to how he had survived the revolt.

"The Jews are a hardy race, intelligent and fanatical with a burning hatred for the Roman and his Empire. They will never be assimilated into our system. They have their own laws and distrust ours. Their diet and social customs forbid them to mix freely with other races. To consort with us is in some way to defile themselves. They will fight viciously and stubbornly and do not fear death.

"However, the Jew is a schemer by nature and a danger when given room to maneuver. They are all individuals, holding tenaciously to their own opinions. They do not have the unquestioning obedience to make a great army. They are a squabbling rabble. A madness has overtaken them; instead of fighting over a wide area in small bands, wearing down the Roman army with constant attacks and lightning retreats, they have chosen to walk like chickens and ducks into a bird coop, the city of Jerusalem, where they scheme against each other. They have already burned most of their own granaries in factional fighting, and have taken all the pilgrims into the city, instead of retaining only fighting men. They are already low on food reserves and have an enormous number of useless mouths to feed. My advice is: throw a wall around the city and watch them peck one another to death like chickens in a coop. The city will fall under its own internal burden.

"As you can see from my plans of the city," Callistus unrolled a very large plan of the city and its defenses under the admiring gaze of the senior commanders and the other officers hopping and squeezing to get a glimpse of the map over each other's shoulders.

"As you can see: the city is fairly easy to defend. The western gate is the weakness, and it would be possible to undermine the tower of Antonia though even this will be extremely difficult. Jerusalem is encompassed by three walls. The other towers are virtually impregnable. I doubt that any siege engines could break them. The stones are huge, closely fitting, and unshakeable. They have their own underground water supply, and they have been creating new cisterns for water storage and collecting rain. They will not die of thirst, but they can soon die of hunger. Here are my estimates of the strength of their army made as I wandered in disguise around the city."

"Well done, well done, Callistus!" shouted Titus, and everyone applauded.

"We shall put you in charge of the siege wall. Now gather all officers to the training ground within the hour. I want to speak to them. Have my platform put in a place where they can all hear me."

The officers dispersed to collect their juniors and gathered in the training ground. It was a hollow surrounded by a ring of rocky crags and formed a natural amphitheatre.

"Commanders and fellow officers," began Titus, "I will be brief. The time you've all been preparing for will soon be on us. The Roman army and Roman citizens have suffered insult and atrocity. The time to avenge that crime is now here. We must show no mercy. The Jews must learn to see and understand what a terrible crime they have committed and they must taste the full rigor of Roman vengeance. We must teach such a lesson that no other group within our empire will even think of insurrection for fear of the what is going to happen here. I repeat, I want no mercy. Anybody accepting bribes or inducements to allow escape shall share the fate of the victim. This includes senior commanders, officers, and men. I want unquestioning obedience from you. I alone bear responsibility to the Roman gods for our actions here. May Jupiter and Mars give us victory."

Under the direction of the senior commanders the officers gave their well-tuned shout of acceptance and the group dispersed, each to carry Titus's message to their own men.

Another council of senior commanders met to discuss immediate strategy.

"You say the western side is the weakest, Callistus," mused Titus as he studied the map in detail. "We shall launch an attack there tomorrow to test their resolve."

"Do not attack for too long. sir," said Callistus quietly. "Prolonged attack may make them, in their fear, forget their differences. We must let internal dissension destroy them."

"I take your point, Callistus." replied Titus. "But right now our own men need action to give them focus and direction. They need to taste enemy blood. Prolonged idleness is bad for them. It can rot an army faster than a piece of meat in a dung hill."

The next day brushwood was rolled forward to fill in the hollows and covered with earth and small stones to make a temporary roadway. Light towers and ladders were carried forward. Archers with engines for shooting arrows and stones mounted the towers, the sides at the top being protected by tightly rolled cloth and covered in tough hide. The towers were wetted and covered on three sides by tightly rolled straw that had been soaked for a long time in water to prevent the defenders from setting the towers on fire. Roman soldiers with shields, in close order protected the flanks of the roadway.

To the blowing of bugles, teams of ladder bearers rushed down the roadway carrying long ladders. While some held onto ropes tied higher up the ladders to prevent the defenders from pushing the ladders away from the walls, others, armored on head, shoulders, neck, and arms, rushed up the ladders, their short swords trying to fend off the spears of the defenders. Once under the spears, they mounted quickly and forced the battlements. The speed of the attack surprised the defenders, and other defenders with short swords and long knives moved in. The defending spearmen sought to pierce the undefended legs of the attackers wherever they could find an opportunity. A hot skirmish developed on the battlements. More ladders were rushed forward while archers on both sides launched arrow after arrow. The Roman siege towers were much taller than the battlements, and many of the defenders' arrows and javelins fell short. Many defenders died under the darts of the attackers from the towers. The battlements lay strewn with the bodies of the dead and wounded.

The plans laid by the defenders during construction of the roadway were brought into action. Two large sorties made their way out of the city to converge on the roadway from both sides. Spear-men presented a front of sharp spikes opposite the soldiers; another line extended out at a right angle where the line of soldiers along the roadway ended. Brushwood was brought, dumped and pushed by spears to create a temporary wall cutting off the Roman's retreat back to their own lines. The brushwood was ignited to create a wall of fire to prevent reinforcements from rushing down the roadway.

Other groups followed, carrying closely woven baskets filled with finely ground sulphur, Arabian naphtha, and quicklime. Water was added, and then the baskets were hurled over the heads of the soldiers onto the roadway. The heat from the moistened quicklime ignited the sulphur and naphtha, and they began to burn fiercely. The flame distracted the soldiers as the heat hit them. A rush of spearmen broke the lines, and other groups rushed forward with more Greek fire; water was added and it was then hurled into the base of the towers. Brushwood from the road was also thrown in. The fierce heat dried the straw, and that too began to burn along with the timbers of the towers. The archers were soon consumed in flames most jumping to their deaths from the tops of the towers, screaming and on fire. Jars of oil were poured onto the roadway taken in through the gaps made by the spearmen and ignited with burning pitch. As the road blazed, the Roman soldiers, unable to fight as a unit, fell prey to the spearmen surrounding them. The attackers' ladders were torn from the walls, and either broken or carried back to the gates by the rapidly retreating sorties. Gates were opened at the last minute, and the bands went back inside the city. The fighting continued for some time on top of the walls until one by one the attackers were either killed or wounded, their armor and weapons were stripped from them and then they were thrown from the walls. Quiet drifted over the battlefield as the Roman army slowly surveyed the scene before them. The whole operation had been carried out too quickly for the Roman army to issue new commands and bring in adequate reinforcements.

"I want rapid day and night attacks," Titus shouted to his commanders. "They must not be able to sleep peacefully. Train the wall attackers to retreat more rapidly down the ladders at the bugle signal. Build a wall of equal height in the camp and train them. I want more archers and cavalry to deal with the sorties. We too can use fire, and we have more supplies of that commodity than they have. Have fast horsemen to hurl burning faggots at them. Train them, train them. The archers were pathetic. They must fire more rapidly and more accurately. They were far too slow. Make an example of the slowest. That should put fire into their bellies, so that they don't allow fire to fall on their comrades. Make outer defenses for the roadways so that they can be defended laterally. I want those roadways built more quickly. Build several at the same time so that they never know which ones we'll use. Level the ground around the city as far as possible so that we can get to the walls more rapidly. Defend the work-men with spear-men and cavalry. Have signalers ready to call for help if needed. Have reinforcements on standby at all times. Bring me Callistus."

Callistus entered the tent of Titus and was offered wine. Following the sweep of Titus's hand he sat to his right.

"An army very soon gets rusty. Did I miss anything in my last instructions, Callistus?"

"As a longer term measure, sir, how about starting mining tunnels to some of the walls and towers? It creates a mood of expectation and hope among the men, and the noise of tunneling is very unnerving to the defenders. It is going to be a long haul, and so we may need emphasis on camp hygiene. In this hot weather diseases break out rapidly particularly if care is not taken with the fresh water. Drinking water must be kept from stagnat-ing. Still or dead water causes pestilence. Water must be poured continually through sand to keep it alive and fresh."

"What materials do you intend to use for the siege wall, Callistus?"

"Layers of staves laid at right angles, and earth and stone between the layers and in the interstices. In that way it's almost impossible to batter them down."

"I have read Julius Caesar's Gallic Wars too. But we have here something a little bit bigger than Avaricum. We are not going to get any rainstorm to help us either. Who is their Vercingetorix, Callistus?"

"They don't seem to have one, sir. They have a war council and subordinate war councils. They seem to be torn with division and factions. One group occupies the Temple area; their leader seems to be one called Simon. Another, led by one called John—

occupying the city—is in uneasy alliance with the Idumeans. They are all intent on controlling the Temple area. You can expect fighting when pilgrims are allowed in during the festival days. Zealots and robber bands wander the city causing great affliction to the people; some of them are extremely corrupt and without shame. They kill people in the street without apparent cause. The defenders will not respond rapidly to changing tactics, as no one will take responsibility for important decisions and the councils take too long to deliberate and co-ordinate their defense. They distrust each other. Rapid movement and changes of tactics will cause the divisions to increase within them, while they argue over counter moves and over whether they can trust their changing allies to support them in distress. Hatreds will get more intense as they get hungrier and more desperate. At all costs the population must be kept in the city. The more mouths they have to feed the sooner they'll get hungry and surrender. I would not risk our men unnecessarily in heroic attacks: just enough to keep them busy constantly and to keep our troops fit and alert. Let time do the rest."

"I have already given instructions that all escapees shall be crucified in sight of and, if possible, within sound of the inhabitants. We shall let fear do its work. Thank you Callistus: the gods have favored us in protecting you for our work now."

## In the City

Reuben had chosen to stay in the city in order to safeguard his possessions and had hired guards to defend the granaries. He and Nicodemus, his friend and a friend of his cousin Joseph, were the major suppliers of grain to the city. Food would soon become the only recognizable currency.

He watched the closing of the gates with the arrival of the Roman legions. Earlier he had watched the burning of most of their granaries by the mob.

His guards were just numerous enough to cause hesitancy among his enemies and prevent them attacking him. There were other weaker groups for them to pillage, and Reuben did not go out of his way to provoke them.

"Reuben and Nicodemus are appeasers; they will use their power over food supplies to control the revolution and they will make a peace treaty with the Romans. It is better for us to starve than give in to an appeaser."

The Zealots burned Reuben's and Nicodemus's granaries to keep control of the revolution and thereby sealed their own fate.

As the siege progressed, Reuben watched with growing apprehension the growth of the wall around the outside of Jerusalem. The Romans intended to starve out the population. The Jewish defenders were now taking food from the inhabitants by force, and this violence could only get worse. His guards were beginning to defect to other more vigorous groups who were getting more of the plunder. Reuben would soon be unable to pay them or to bribe them for their loyalty. He would not allow them to go on pillaging expeditions.

Reuben now had no future in Jerusalem. He would soon be killed, as had many other rivals in the struggle for leadership and direction of the siege. He decided to escape before the outer wall was complete. He had read of the terrible tactics the Romans used in siege warfare.

On a dark night, he slipped over the wall covered with a dark cloak. He went slowly from memory to the place where he thought the wall was most incomplete. A gully had hindered the building of the wall in that sector. He was now too old to scale a wall by rope.

As he neared what he thought was the gully he decided to wait until dawn for a little more light to see his way and to avoid any Roman soldiers.

In the dark he had not moved near enough to the gully; and so he crawled along the bottom of the wall covering himself with his cloak and avoiding looking up since the flash of his eyes or teeth might be seen from the ramparts.

He had been spotted.

As he crawled up the gully a sword touched the back of his neck. Reuben kept all four of his limbs on the ground.

"There is gold for you if you let me through, my friend," muttered Reuben, just loud enough for his captor to hear.

"Stand up slowly and keep your hands away from your body. . . .Where is the gold?"

"In the pouch attached to my belt."

"Untie it with one hand and throw it behind you."

Reuben did that . . . and was then stunned with a blow, and his arms and legs were pinioned.

He was thrown into a group of others captured that morning.

There were so many prisoners that the Romans did not bother to flog them all before crucifixion. But those who resisted were flogged in front of the others until they lost the will to resist.

When Reuben's turn came they told him to lie on the ground face upwards and stretch his arms sideways. A rope noose was fitted around each wrist; at a word of command two teams of men pulled his arms apart, a wooden beam was fitted under his shoulder blades, and his arms below the elbow were tied to the beam. A smaller rope was also fixed to his upper arm to stop him from wriggling free from his bonds. The beam was then hauled to an upright and slotted into place and secured with ropes. The teams worked quickly.

Reuben did not yet feel the pain. That would come later.

He had a clear view of the city of Jerusalem. The position had been chosen carefully. The Romans wanted to terrorize the inhabitants into staying in the city and so shorten the siege by starvation.

As he looked at the city Reuben began to sing the psalm

Welcome sound when I heard them saying,
"We will go into the Lord's house!"
Within thy gates Jerusalem,
Our feet stand at last;
Jerusalem built as a city should be built
That is one in fellowship.

There the tribes meet,
The Lord's own tribes,
To give praise,
As Israel is ever bound
To the Lord's name;
There the thrones are set for judgment,
Thrones for the house of David.
Pray for all that brings Jerusalem peace!
May all who love Thee dwell at ease,
Let there be peace within thy ramparts,
Ease in thy strongholds!"

A passing soldier picked up a handful of dust and flung it with all his might into Reuben's eyes.

Reuben panicked when he suddenly realized he could do nothing to clear his eyes.

He struggled to continue.

"For love of my brethren and my familiar friends,
Peace is still my prayer for Thee;
Remembering the house of the Lord our God,
For thy happiness I plead."

Through his tears and pain, Reuben could make out a horse that had stopped facing him.

"Wipe that man clean!"

A leper took a box, stood on it, wiped Reuben's eyes and whispered in his ear:

"He is Callistus the Roman, and he is doing an act of kindness.

"I am Stephas, a priest of the Christians, and we are here to tend to the dying. Callistus is risking his life . . .

"I know you . . . you are related to Joseph's family" continued the leper. "Have you received baptism?"

"No."

"Do you want to receive baptism? Baptism will take away all sins from your soul, and you shall be with the Lord, your God, this day in Paradise."

Reuben remembered the look that Mary had given him after the baptism of David, and the memory of her face remained in his imagination.

"I want to do the will of God with all my heart."

"That is enough. I shall pronounce the words over you, while I baptize you with water."

Reuben felt the cool refreshing water on his face and head as he was bathed with a sponge. The memory of Mary's face still lingered.

"Nice timing, Mary: minimum time when I could sin. Please keep me away from sin and despair until I die."

"Has he been cleaned?" shouted Callistus.

"Yes, sir."

Reuben could now see Callistus leaning forward on his horse in front of him.

"Nice day."

It took an effort for Reuben to say it steadily.

"It is for some, not for me" replied Callistus.

Reuben took the double irony and nodded.

"I offer my body in atonement for sin especially mine and for success in the mission that the Lord has entrusted to Joseph, my cousin. I consider it an honor for me to die in the same manner as Christ. Death on a cross must be important for the redemption of man, otherwise God the Son, would not have freely chosen to die in such a way." Reuben's body sank exhausted.

Callistus could see that all the muscles in Reuben's body were beginning to tremble the beginning of the excruciating agony that would last for eight to ten hours until death brought release.

"I recognize this man!" shouted Callistus. "He is a rich man, he will have swallowed gold and jewels."

Knives were soon cutting through Reuben's blood vessels; he lost consciousness, dropping gently into the arms of Abraham.

Callistus waited until the last of the disappointed jackals had left Reuben's body, and then shouted.

"Remove that body . . . we need the space!"

The lepers complied, placed the remains of Reuben's body on a large cloth and removed it for burial, led by the priest.

"You're a strange one," remarked a centurion, who had watched the proceedings.

"I've seen many forms of enjoyment in the death of prisoners, but I've never seen wiping them with leprosy before now. What a strange vengeance! Describe to me sometime the enjoyment you get out of it."

"They are cleaner than you, my dirty little friend" muttered Callistus. "Remember me, Reuben, in your kingdom . . . help me make sense of this mad-house of a world. Why am I here? And what am I supposed to do?"

Callistus turned his horse and went back to supervising the construction of the ramparts.

The siege took months, long periods of languid waiting, frenetic activity during a raid, excited talk afterwards as new refinements and strategies were devised, then long periods of more silence. Occasionally, during the night, screams could be heard coming from the city.

People tried to escape the city in increasing numbers. The older ones and the weak were pushed out of the city. None escaped: none survived. Wood became very scarce for the manufacture of crosses; they ringed the city.

Eventually the tunnels undermined the tower and walls, and one of the walls came crashing to the ground. Roman soldiers gradually captured one wall after another. They demolished the Antonia tower: the Temple cloisters were burned and eventually the silver gates of the temple. Then the Temple itself was burned, and hope went out of the people. The defenders were too weak to rebuild, and the remainder of the city fell to the final all-out assault.

# CHAPTER 31

## ꩜ Simon's Story

Simon slept restlessly. Strong sunlight was streaming through the shutters. It was already hot, and he had a headache. He could hear his father shouting. With reluctance he decided to get up. He slouched untidily into the living room, sat on a bench near the table and reached out for the wine and water. He poured out some wine, added water, and drank noisily.

His father who was taking late morning refreshment, eyed him cynically. Simon was used to his father's displeasure and took no notice. Some work on the farm was given to him, and he nodded without comment.

Sometimes his father would get angry, particularly if some mishap had occurred on the farm, and Simon would be forced to get up early. On those occasions he would follow his father and then, when he had been left alone with the work that needed to be done, he found the shade of a tree or bush or wall and resumed his interrupted sleep. In late afternoon when he was bored, he would get up and work quickly to complete the tasks he had been given. This would at least work up an appetite for the evening meal. His father was ashamed of Simon's shoddy workmanship and often complained bitterly to his friends. They nodded but said nothing, conscious that making comments about family is always a dangerous thing to do in the countryside.

Simon was fed up with farm life. The slow cycle, the tedium, and the hardness of the day-to-day routine bored him. Often as he lay in the shade, he dreamed of life in the city with all its excitements. There he would be respected; there he would be able to achieve his full potential. He resented the fact that his father did not respect him. His mother loved him and was desperately afraid of losing his love. He knew how to flatter her when he wanted some concession. He could talk to his mother, but not to his father. If his father refused him something, he could always get it from his mother—sometimes clandestinely. He only needed to threaten loss of affection for his mother to give in to his demands. When his father found out from time to time that his will had been thwarted by his wife, he would go into rages. This cycle led to a lot of friction in the household.

Recently he had needed more money. His girlfriend Ozira lived in a nearby village; and he had liked her. He had made her pregnant, but had delayed the betrothal despite her pleas because he wanted time to think. Marriage would commit him forever to farm life, and he didn't want that. Anyway her pregnancy was discovered and she was killed by her father and angry relatives. She had never disclosed the identity of the father, although suspicion had rested on him. Because of this episode he had decided to get his comforts from Gischala, the nearest town. Love cost money there, but it had less dangers and complications. He found that these town women were better at the love talk than he had been with Ozira; but there was an element of theater about it. Underneath, he thought he detected a hatred, a hatred for men—all of them. Still, their opinions did not concern him. Getting back at night or early morning involved a long walk back to his village, and the walk exhausted him. He was often very tired in the morning and this tiredness made his father angry. Things were reaching crisis point, and even he realized that he must do something. Things could not go on this way forever. He decided to leave before he was thrown out.

He made his plans. He went to the house of his grandparents while they were eating with his parents. He lifted the tile in the living room and took out the earthenware pot. As a small child, he had seen them dropping coins into this pot. He emptied out the pot into his large pouch, and then filled the pot to the same height with small stones. He then poured some of the coins back on top, spaced them with his fingers to hide the stones, lowered the pot back into the hole, and replaced the tile.

He reasoned thus: his grandparents were old, and with their poor eyesight would never notice the missing money. The money would only go to his father on their death, and he had no respect for his father. When he had made money in the city, then he could always help his parents.

He left that night for Jerusalem. He had already packed his belongings and had hidden them in a field near the house. He left a note for his mother telling her his intentions and telling her not to worry. The money was securely in his pouch tied to his belt.

When he arrived at Jerusalem he was wide-eyed with astonishment at the number of people, the size and grandeur of the buildings, and the variety of goods for sale. He found lodgings in a poor part of the city. He was not so foolish as to waste money. He realized that his money would not last forever and soon set about looking for a job. But the poor rates of pay and the long hours appalled him. When he recounted his experience to prospective employers he was met with derision. His accent and his rural innocence amused them. But he was strongly built and eventually found work collecting gambling debts for one of the dice houses near where he lived. The pay was poor, but it didn't involve getting up early in the morning. He went around with others just in case of trouble from unwilling payers. Often a threat was enough. Although it was dangerous if caught, he was told to carry a knife. He was told to hide it if there were Romans about, since carrying a knife carried a stiff penalty.

Thus Simon gradually slipped into city ways and began to find his way about the city. He didn't like cooking. His mother had always cooked for him, so he used to buy from stalls selling hot food in the street. He was living slightly beyond his means; but until he could make his fortune, he could dig into his savings. He always carried his money around with him.

One afternoon he had got up hungry and decided to go and get something to eat. He had not bothered to get out his money first because he was hungry. When he arrived at the stall and bought the food he found he had no money in his pocket, and so he tipped some coins out of his pouch into his hand, paid for the food and put the change back into his pouch. But he had been seen. While he was walking along eating his food he was jostled rather roughly by some boys running laughing down the street. He went on walking back to his room in order to prepare for his evening work. Then he noticed the cut laces of his pouch. The pouch itself was gone. Simon did not go to work that evening, but lay on his bed as waves of rage passed over him. His anger and frustration knew no bounds. He hated the people of Jerusalem. Their arrogance and contempt for country people had stung him, and now this.

Since the people of Jerusalem had stolen money from him, then he must get it back. But how? He must plan. He was now much more afraid of losing his job since he had no money. His inability to buy little luxuries made him suffer. His planning became urgent. In his visits to clients he began to take note of the layout of the houses. He sometimes watched as the inhabitants wandered around their homes. Every house had to have a hiding place. He began to see patterns. Most people tended to have the same kind of hiding places: something that would not be affected by fire, that meant the ground floor; something solid, that meant either a fire place, a stove, or an end wall. A hole in the floor covered with a carpet was the favorite. The next favorite was under the hearth stone. He often could see the claw marks where the stone had been lifted.

Simon chose his time carefully: late afternoon on his way to work. He slipped into the house of a client he had visited some months previously; there was now no reason to link him with the theft. He lifted the hearthstone easily since there was no fire lit;

he reached his hand into the hole and put a fistful of contents into his shoulder bag. He thought for a moment and then reached in again. He lowered the stone carefully and made his way to the back door. A sound outside made him hesitate to open the door. Just then the latch lifted, and Simon just had time to hide behind the door. The door closed, and Simon froze. He was level with his client's shoulder. Instead of turning away from Simon to go into the room the client turned right and almost stepped on Simon. A look of surprise and recognition, and then a pause, and then realizing what was happening he began to shout and make a grab for Simon. The shouting made Simon put his hand over the man's mouth, and he was promptly bitten. The shouting resumed until Simon's knife entered under his ribs, and he fell to the floor. Simon calmly walked out into the street through the front door, though his body was shaking terribly. He still had the presence of mind to go to work having first carefully checked that he had no blood marks.

It was with pleasure that he looked through his haul the following morning. He even got up early as soon as it was light. He had more than recovered his loss. Simon felt that justice had been done, and he had recovered his lost rights. He made sure that he never again carried all his wealth with him but thought carefully how to hide his possessions in different locations to minimize loss. He would be cleverer than his clients.

After a few days his nerves calmed and he began to enjoy life again. The brooding moodiness and depression gradually left him after a few nights of drinking.

He decided to dispose of some of the trinkets he had gathered in his haul. He thought first of getting rid of an amulet and chain and decided to take it to a seller of gold and silver objects to see how much he could get for it.

He told the shopkeeper that it had been in his family but that he needed some money, and he asked how much he would give him for it. He wasn't foolish but tried a couple of shops to compare offers. The last one made a good offer but the shopkeeper said he needed to check to see if the gold was genuine. While the shopkeeper was at the back of the shop two more customers entered. He waited, and then the shop keeper returned. "You know I think I recognize this piece. I think I sold this just a few weeks ago. You say it's been in your family for some time, but it's a modern design. The person I sold it to was murdered. Simon's arms were grasped by the two customers behind him as he reached for his knife. He was propelled by the men to the yard at the back of the shop, and his wrists were tied. He was made to sit on a low stool. After some hours of waiting in the sun a man of rather slow, dignified bearing made his appearance. The cloth of his headband partly covered his face.

"It is a terrible thing to be a robber and a murderer. The Romans have horrible punishments for those who are caught. We will show you their execution site later.

"We are faced with alternatives. We can hand you over to the Romans, or kill you ourselves: our ways are more humane. Or you could do a job for us. You are a patriot, aren't you?" Simon nodded. The options pointed him in that direction.

"We have a man of similar age to the one you killed, but he is not so pleasant a person. He is an informer, an informer for the Romans, and we want him out of the way. We want you to kill him. Do you agree to our proposal?" Simon nodded. He really had no choice.

Simon wandered through the crowd with an accomplice. When the accomplice rubbed his nose, it was an indication as to the intended victim. The process was repeated with different accomplices until Simon was certain of the identity of the victim. He was then told to watch his movements until a good opportunity presented itself. Simon's patience was rewarded. The victim on Friday nights used to visit a particular little house on a quiet street off a busy thoroughfare in the city. He gave a double-three series of knocks, before being admitted. Twice Simon hid behind a pile of tanned leather at the end of the street as he watched the ritual entry. He checked the distance between his hiding place and the doorway, and the time needed to get there; he even practiced the knife thrust.

The execution of the task was easier than he thought. He knifed him before he even started his knock, so that Simon was well clear before his body was discovered slumped in the doorway.

There were words of praise from his masters. He was invited to a training camp outside Jerusalem. There he learned some of the tactics of the Sicarii. His next assignment was to assassinate a Roman soldier who had been particularly brutal with the local population. Simon was petrified. He listened intently as points of entry into the body were pointed out to him; quick kills, silent kills, kills against an opponent defending himself, and those fast quick unexpected kills which leave little or no blood on the assailant and so make identification difficult later. Soldiers wore armor and so the blade had to go underneath and it had to be quick. Roman soldiers never went around the city on their own; they went in pairs and often within calling distance of other groups in case of trouble. One slip of mistiming and Simon faced an excruciating death. Simon was sick with fear. At nights he lay sleepless and sweating. He practiced and practiced, and ran and ran, to make his running faster. He had never worked so hard in his life. In moment of silence, the thoughts came flooding in, churning around inside his head and vibrating his bowels. He thought about praying. Ozira had been of religious inclination, but he didn't want to be reminded of her now. He focused on the task ahead.

On the morning of the assassination attempt, Simon got up early. He couldn't sleep. He put on his country cloak and walked around in the morning air until dawn. The knife would be waiting for him in the city, which he set out for as soon as there was light. On entering the city he was searched by a guard at the gate. He drifted through the city to his appointed meeting place. The knife would be behind some water jars. He felt behind the jars, and his fingers touched the blade. He slid his fingers along until he found the handle. Then he casually looked around and quietly slipped the weapon under his cloak and into the pocket in the folds. He tested it several times for ease of withdrawal and concealment. A diversion would be created to give him some opportunity for the knife stroke so that he could be away before anyone realized what was happening.

The soldier had been pointed out to him previously. Two of them stood at the edge of the market square. Simon moved to within easy running distance of the closest one. He also mentally planned his escape route. There was no going back. He was told that if he messed up on this job he would be killed. He knew too much already. What he didn't know was that other assassins had been appointed to kill him if it looked as if he would be captured. It would appear that irate citizens, capturing a robber, had clubbed him and broken his neck.

Simon waited, trying not to look at his victim and arouse suspicion. Suddenly a cart full of metal utensils clattered to the ground as two carts got their wheels hooked together and the animals bolted. Simon ran forward took out his knife at the last minute and plunged the knife under the right rib of the victim and up into the heart. He pulled the knife out quickly and ran to a side street. He pounded down the street and stuck the knife into a cart of dried dung parked there. Then he stopped running, looked carefully at his clothes for blood marks, and then joined the crowd in the street heading for the city gates. He felt tremendous relief when he got out into the fields and groves north of Jerusalem; as though a huge weight had been lifted from his heart. He almost danced his way back to the camp and was wreathed in smiles when he greeted his companions. For safety they moved camp immediately. The celebration that night was stupendous. They all got thoroughly drunk, as Simon told and retold what had happened. They tried not to think about the reprisals going on in the city. Later they found out that the soldier had died without a sound and that no one was sure how the killing had taken place or who had done it. This earned special praise from the master. Simon was respected now.

The revolt in Jerusalem started soon afterwards. Simon re-entered the city when Herod's armory at Massada was broken open and the garrison of Romans were massacred after being promised safe passage. Simon was also present in the pursuit of

Cestius, who first tried to take the city and then was forced to retreat, through lack of provisions, to Bethoron. He witnessed the massacre of the Roman rearguard.

He also took part in the raiding parties to the surrounding towns, collecting provisions for the defense of the city. His knowledge of hiding places enabled him to collect items useful for his wealth, after the trouble was over. He hid his treasures in various parts of the city; some of his favorite hiding places were under derelict gravestones.

When John, the rebel leader, entered the city after his escape from the siege of Gischala, Simon met many of his fellow countrymen. He enquired about his family, but no one could tell him whether they were alive or not. He thought of leaving the city and going back to his own part of the country, but he now had many valuables in the city. He would be able to go back a reasonably wealthy man, and he would be respected. At the moment, carts were in very short supply. Even if he did manage to get one, he would never be able to make his way back to his home territory alone. His cart would be confiscated by one of the robber bands roaming the countryside, or it would be stolen by one of the many farmers in the region who had had their own possessions taken. He would never be able to defend it alone, especially if it were full of valuables. He would have to wait for the return of law and order; then he would take his possessions bit by bit over a long period of time so as not to arouse suspicion. Then he changed his mind about leaving. Jerusalem was so mighty a city, with so many people to defend it that he thought there wasn't an army in the whole world big enough to take it.

No, he would be safer in the city until things got better.

Simon did not join John's party immediately. There was a lot of fighting between the various groups and there was no point in risking his life needlessly. He was hired by Reuben to defend his granaries. He met him by chance. He always had had a loathing for lepers. He had seen them, horribly deformed, roaming the countryside after they had been expelled from cities or towns. He had seen some of them dead and unburied in country lanes. One of them had come close to him outside the city and he had thrown a rock at him. But then Reuben came by and was kind to the leper, so Simon went up to Reuben and apologized. He knew him to be a rich man.

Reuben hired him as one of his guards. This gave him employment and access to grain, an important future commodity.

He had stored some of it away before some of the Zealots came to him and threatened what they would do if he prevented their firebrands from entering the granaries. It seems that everyone had his eye on the granaries, and the Zealots were few. If they allowed other groups to take the grain they would be outnumbered and would be unable to attract followers; other groups would be richer and more numerous. They decided to burn the granaries to prevent their being taken by others.

Simon never had taken part in other people's quarrels, and so he looked away as the groups set fire to his granary. He cut and burned himself to give an impression of having fought a good fight.

Later, when the factions stopped fighting among themselves, with the arrival of Titus, their common enemy, at the city gates, Simon joined John's party. They were well armed and therefore would not go short of food.

He was present at the first sortie against the Roman siege engines.

As the sally left the gates he pushed his way into the party defending the gates. It was unwise to go too far from the city gates. He didn't relish the idea of the gates being closed with him on the outside. Slip-ups always occur in this kind of fighting. Later when the party returned he pushed in with them as they came back through the gates, and joined in their celebrations.

The next months were spent in idleness. The huge siege towers, looking down on the walls of the city and covered in plates of iron terrified him. He occasionally joined search parties looking for food among non-combatant elements of the population; desperate and cruel methods often seem necessary in war, and the defenders had to be fed in order to fight.

The loss of the Temple unnerved him. He knew it was just a matter of time before the city fell. The Zealots got together and discussed plans for making a last stand in the lower city. There would be great slaughter since the Romans were enraged and now saw victory in their grasp.

His group was working on some form of defensive arrangement just before the Romans broke into the city. As the cries of the population rose at the entry of the Roman army, Simon noticed his commander slip away. He followed him, making sure that he didn't realize he was being followed. The commander ran down a few side streets, now almost deserted. Simon followed, keeping him within eyesight. The commander stopped near a small street leading to a small rocky outcrop. He looked up and down the thoroughfare and then ran down the street. Simon ran to the street as fast as he could and was just in time to see him disappear into the back yard of a house which adjoined the outcrop. Simon crept up to see some children climbing into a small hole in a wall, the wife followed. At this point Simon ran up and killed the commander with one knife thrust. He slit the throat of the wife while her head was still sticking out of the hole. He then called the children out one by one and killed them. He left the bodies outside. Their corpses would deter any search parties. He then scrambled into the hole and found a cave. The entrance had been cunningly sealed by stone slabs to make it look like a natural wall. Inside an oil lamp flickered; food, oil and water had been stored in jars, enough to last a family through the violent part of the siege. He thought he could quietly escape when city life got back to normal. Simon crawled into the hole and drew in the stone behind him. He then prepared himself for the long wait by the light of a flickering oil lamp. He always took great care when refilling it with oil, lighting another lamp and taking great care in the trimming and replacement of the wick. He did not fancy a long time in total darkness.

As he lay there, from time to time he could hear sounds outside; and then, as he held his breath, he listened to them fade away. How secure he was in the bowels of the earth! The children would never have kept quiet. They would have been captured, and would have met with a horrible death. Their death had been very quick. They had been spared the horrors of war.

Simon gradually lost track of time. He did not know whether it was day or night outside. He tried to use his digestive cycle to count the number of days. His sleep pattern became irregular.

It was during one of those periods of fitful dozing that he was awakened by heavy thumps against the wall of the cave. His heart pounded as a hole was made in the wall, and a burning torch pushed through the hole. There were shouts outside and more pounding as the wall gradually came down. He was ordered out to face a squad of Roman soldiers. It seemed that many of the high-born and wealthy had hidden their treasures in sub-subterranean caverns and crevices in case of a siege of the city. The Romans became expert at finding them. The more the treasure the bigger the entrance, and the easier it was to discover. Simon was bound and led to a group of other prisoners.

Fortunately the Romans had grown tired of killing.

Some lepers were wandering around the group offering to wash away sins and prepare people for the next life. Simon moved away. He loathed lepers and he would need all his wits about him to survive in the times ahead.

He did not want his freedom of action to be curtailed by scruples.

Simon was not kept in the city long but was moved with Titus's legions to Caesarea Philippi. It was a long journey with maddening thirst during the day, and with terrible hunger which never abated. They only drank in the evening when the column stopped for the night. Simon always kept himself in the middle of the group and his back lower than the others to escape the lash and the guards' attention. They were herded into cellars at Caesarea Philippi, and the diet improved.

One afternoon they were led to an arena and told to put on armor. Simon noticed that one group were being more heavily armed than the other and were more numerous. They were being given swords whereas the other group were given only knives. He quietly pushed his way into that group. The group with the knives were led away first.

A Roman guard addressed the group. They were told that they were to re-enact the siege of Jerusalem for the benefit of Titus and the citizens of Caesarea. They were given graphic detail of what would happen to them if they did not fight. They were then led out into the arena to the cheers of the crowd. The defenders were already in place at the top of a huge wooden wall, painted to depict a wall of Jerusalem. The attackers were given wooden ladders. After brief planning the attackers launched themselves forward.

Simon arranged it so that he was not first up the ladder but close behind the leader. When he got to the top of the ladder, he made a rush with all his might for a corner of the parapet between the wall and a mock tower. He crouched down and assumed a porcupine position in the corner. The defenders were soon busy fighting with the attackers coming up the ladder, and Simon watched as they killed each other. When only a small group of attackers remained, he joined them.

They were told to descend the wall and were then disarmed. Groups of archers and foot-soldiers prevented any escape attempt.

While Simon was taking off the last of his armor he was suddenly pushed forward and told to pick up a sword sticking into the sand of the arena. He was then told to kill one of the prisoners in front of him, who was unarmed. Simon rushed forward and killed him before the man could prepare himself. He then stuck the sword in the ground and walked towards the exit, thankful it was all over.

The guards started laughing at him and he couldn't understand why.

As he pushed towards the exit the guards laughed and pushed him back. One of them pointed to the center of the arena.

Simon saw that another prisoner had taken up the sword and was advancing towards him.

He was now the unarmed victim.

There would be a chain of such fights, the winner fighting unarmed against the next in line who had the sword.

An exotic death was reserved for the last one.

Simon yelled and tried to push his way out. One of the guards with a red-hot iron bar, which he used to force reluctant gladiators into the arena, placed the bar under his bottom. Simon yelled and jumped towards his opponent clutching his burn. The crowd let out a huge guffaw.

A wave of anger swept over Simon.

"B-A-S-T-A-R-D-S," He yelled at the top of his voice.

The crowd laughed even more.

"YOU HAVE NO RESPECT."

The spectators found this even more entertaining.

Simon's opponent advanced towards him, and Simon made a grab for the blade. His opponent drew the sword back violently cutting a long slice along Simon's palm and across his fingers.

Simon kicked, and that drew a cheer from the crowd. He kicked again, but this time the kick missed.

Simon parried a slashing blow with his arm, which almost broke his forearm. The same thing happened again, and again Simon parried with his forearm. The pain was intense. Simon reached down and threw sand at his opponents face; but the move was seen and the sand had no effect. Another parry to the forearm.

Simon turned and ran, chased by the opponent.

The crowd laughed.

The intense pain in his arms and the burn on his bottom slowed him down. His days of idleness while hiding had made him unfit.

Simon turned and fell to the sand, raising his legs to keep off his opponent. His legs soon had a multitude of cuts as the sword slashed with increasing vigor.

Simon lay with the stumps of his arms and legs in the air like a slain goat. He could no longer defend himself. A quick leap and the man made a downward stabbing movement to the side of the neck.

Blood began to pump out.

The man didn't give a further death blow. He wanted time to recover in order to fight the next opponent. He left Simon to die from loss of blood

Simon held his gnarled stumps to his neck and focused his mind on the pumping blood. He wanted not to think about anything else. He lay like a child with his arms in a spurting geyser of warm water, saying nothing. Simon vaguely sensed a noose being slipped over his legs and his body being hauled across the sand as he slowly lost consciousness.

Able men had been sorted out for sale as slaves and so were the women. The rest were led for slaughter or to be used in the arenas.

Simon had been one of the unlucky ones, or as some would say later one of the lucky ones.

The price of slaves was so low because of the surplus of prisoners that many able bodied men had become expendable.

## THE LAST DAYS

Stephas and his lepers had been busy giving consolation to the prisoners and baptizing those who chose to be baptized, all under the watchful eye of Callistus.

Titus began to grow suspicious. At a meeting with his senior officers he suddenly turned to Callistus.

"Those lepers have had vengeance enough, Callistus. They are wiping too many with leprosy. They will spread the contagion to my army. Round them up and burn them. Get some Jewish prisoners under threat of crucifixion to do it for you and then burn them along with the lepers."

"I have a debt of honor to them, sir. They saved my life. I hid as one of them during the revolt."

"Mercy is a nice ornament for women, Callistus, but not for a Roman soldier. They are Jews and they are lepers. They are doubly defiled. Burn them. Otherwise you share the same fate. No one carries the conscience of Rome but me. I make the moral decisions here. I made that clear from the beginning. The security of the Empire demands that we be brutal and that we are seen to be brutal."

"Sir, the Jews have a story that a man called Moses, after long conversation with their God, came down Mount Sinai with two tablets of stone on which were written ten commandments-three of them governing relations with God himself and the other seven governing relations with our neighbor. They were written in stone to show that they were laws eternal, for all time, as long as man dwells on earth. They came down from Mount Sinai, symbolizing that they are laws not from human wisdom but prescribed by God himself. They cannot be broken if man is to bear his own name with honor.

"Each man and woman has a face which is unique; there is never any other identical one, neither now, nor in the past nor in the future. The face mirrors the soul, and that also is unique. There will never be another like it. Each man is in control of his own soul, his own kingdom, and is beholden to no other. His soul relates to God alone, not to man.

"I defend the empire of Rome, but I defend my own kingdom first. This inner kingdom is in my charge; and mine alone. Rome is strong because of its justice, and I will not stain it."

"You are a madman, Callistus. At my side, Rome and its Empire will be at your feet. Your name will be famous within its boundaries for all time. You shall set the law.

"No law is greater than the lawgiver. That is why emperors are gods. You shall beget the law for me, and only you can break it. Yet, you have defied me in front of my officers. I am your lawgiver. Recant. And all will be forgotten. I have great plans for you, Callistus. Don't be foolish and become a nobody. Everybody needs powerful friends and I will be that friend to you. Do as I say. I want to hear no more about it."

"I need to enter my kingdom with my own name, sir. I cannot."

Titus froze. He looked at Callistus intently.

"Burn him along with the others. I don't want his contagion to spread to my commanders, neither physical leprosy nor mental." Titus turned and left.

The guards moved to bind Callistus but he turned to them and said: "No need," and walked with them to await execution.

It took less than an hour to round up the lepers and they were chained at the foot along with the Jewish soldiers who had gathered them in. Brushwood was piled around them with a narrow passageway through the brush to the center stake where the chain had been anchored. The centurion in charge of execution finally indicated to Callistus to walk down the pathway in the brushwood to the center. The center of the training ground had been chosen as the place of execution, and many officers and soldiers were there to watch. Word of the confrontation had passed quickly around the camp.

Before entering the pathway a young centurion stopped him, just when Callistus was out of earshot of the others. The centurion had chosen his moment carefully.

"May I have your ring, sir."

"Why do you want it, because of its value?" asked Callistus.

"Oh no, sir; as a memento. I was present at your confrontation with Titus. I had a Jewish nurse as a child, and she told me stories from their book. She encouraged me to learn the Ten Commandments by heart, and I still remember them. That is why I understood a little of what you said."

Callistus passed the ring to him without the others seeing and then said "Get into contact with the followers of Jesus, a Jew, who was crucified in Jerusalem. You will find what they have to say interesting."

"That won't be possible, sir. I have been commissioned to Britain to safeguard the metal trade for the Roman army. My family name is Albanus; yet it is your name that shall be passed to my children and my children's children. I shall not forget your name, sir, nor the memory of your face. If it would not be too dangerous or imprudent, I would like to kiss it. We shall have to content ourselves with a mental kiss. May the God of Israel take you to his kingdom, sir, for ever and ever."

"May God walk with you in Britain, Albanus."

Callistus stood and waited in the center of the brushwood.

"Where is this cleansing water of yours, Stephas? Isn't it time you gave me some?"

Callistus knelt as Stephas poured the water over his head from the small leper water jar hooked on his belt, and repeated the words of baptism.

A guffaw came from the officers and soldiers with the fire brands.

"You will need more water than they have to offer to protect you from the fire we have ready for you, Callistus," shouted one of them.

"It is not from this fire that I need to protect myself, but from the everlasting fires of Hades, destined for those who follow the ways of wickedness and cowardice. I die for God and for justice, Roman justice and the justice of God, who also rules.

"'Jesus imperat, Jesus vincit; Jesus rules, Jesus conquers.' Take care of yourselves; an everlasting fire awaits you unless you change. Make contact with the Christ followers, so that you may have your sins forgiven. Remember my words when the opportunity comes."

Callistus stood until the flames engulfed him.

The tenth legion was designated to stay behind with the slave workers in a camp near the Western Wall. They demolished the whole city except for three towers to a depth of several feet. Large quantities of valuables were uncovered which had been buried by the city's wealthy.

# CHAPTER 32

## ❧ Karen

The letter from David did not contain news of the death of Reuben.

With the death of Rebecca, contact with relatives had been lost; and in the confusion of the siege, and the consequent dispersion, each was concerned with his own immediate relatives.

David's letter was read out in all the villages, and offers came in to replace the Jerusalem Temple with buildings dedicated to the Lord in each of the villages where the true God was worshipped.

Joseph had a few grains of the Holy Ground mounted behind polished sections of jade, blue stone from deep in the heart of Britain, or agate or quartz or other precious stones. Each was given to a village that had a building dedicated to the Lord, and it was placed under the altar where the Eucharist was to be celebrated.

The father of Antonius, Marcellus Glabrio, came to visit Joseph; and, although not a Christian, offered two stone buildings for worship in the new religion.

Joseph agreed, but asked that they be built in Roman style and be called *Aedificatio Conventi*—or meeting houses.

"The Romans are less likely to destroy something which is built like their own and bears a name common to them," Joseph thought.

Marcellus imported specialists in mosaics and had the interior designed with imperial designs, something he was allowed to do being of a distinguished family. They became respected buildings, and Antonius was able to make much progress with the Roman immigrants, who came to govern the new province or for trade.

Roman traders and merchants came in increasing numbers from Gaul, especially in work related to metals, grain, and fish. They naturally met at or near the meeting houses, and Antonius made friends with them.

The high-born British and the Romans tended to worship in the new Roman buildings, but the poorer members of the faithful tended to worship among their own in the wooden Churches.

This separation disturbed Joseph, and he made efforts to worship among his old friends, whose language was British.

Eleanor was already deeply engrossed in organizing the Christian women in their care for slaves and the neglected; she only contacted the stone Churches to ask for money and help.

The little group grew and prospered, and many Roman children made friends with British children of their own age. Roman and British became interchangeable in the language of the towns, particularly in the commercial districts.

Karen's letter came first, carried by another of the desert Christians.

*"Dearest Father, love of my life,*

*"I am filled with joy to hear of your survival and the wonderful work being carried out on the edge of the world.*

*"How often I used to tug your beard when you held me in your arms, your kindly eyes shining like carriage lamps as you held me. Now I tug your beard and kiss you a thousand times even though the distance be great; for those who love, distance is of no importance.*

*"I pray for you daily, and have done that ever since you were so cruelly separated from us. I have dedicated myself to the Lord and his Will, with Mary as my guide; and she it was who directed me to work in Upper Egypt.*

*"The temples here are breathtaking in their splendor and their religion has many features which make it easy for them to understand our Way. The number of conversions to the Lord has reached staggering proportions, and we don't know how to cope.*

*"The imperial household of Ethiopia is encouraging us to come, but we are weighed down with baptisms and instruction, and there are few of us to deal with such a burden. But the load is sweet and pleasing to the Lord and we are content.*

*"David tells me that the conversions in Britain are few but steadfast and that you look like a big mountain bear. That's my daddy, hairy beard sticking out of the body of a bear. I would love to crush you in my own embrace, but will have to rest content with showering you with the dew of my prayers.*

*"David has left for Corinth and sends his love. I shall write as often as I can, once we have found ways of getting our messages to you.*

> *"Your loving daughter,*
> *"Karen."*

Another long letter detailed her life since Joseph's parting.

Karen, the younger daughter, was the most affectionate. Like her mother, she had an artistic temperament. Quick and spontaneous in affection, she also had a quick temper, especially when teased by her older sister.

She delighted in praise but suffered terribly when people chastised her. Although not very academic in intellect, she was sharp and practical and had a good business head. She was a born organizer and soon had people involved in helping her in her enterprises.

Reuben was her slave, and she held him with bonds of affection which he was unwilling to break. She was the apple of his eye.

Her education had been thorough and her writing and design skills had been carefully developed. Her drawings adorned the walls of her room and most of the rooms of the house, and were posted everywhere in Reuben's apartments in Jerusalem. Reuben watched the growing maturity in her work with interest. He planned to have an exhibition someday.

Ruth had left home first, to go to the Parthians some six years after Joseph's departure. Karen stayed at home for another four years.

When asked to go to Alexandria by one of the holy women, she volunteered immediately. The disciples had already established a small group in that town.

She had not been in Alexandria long when she befriended two girls from upper Egypt who were attending the same language school. They were learning Greek. She was learning Egyptian. Both girls were daughters of cloth merchants in upper Egypt, so that when the disciples decided to go to upper Egypt, she was chosen to take a group of girls including the now Christian Egyptian girls with them. Reuben had been co-opted to market Egyptian cloth and paper. He had levered his business associates into marketing her wares, and she had been quick to alter designs to suit the home markets. She already had a flourishing business by the time of her move to upper Egypt.

She funded most of the Christian enterprises in upper Egypt and she regularly sailed up and down the Nile in connection with business. After an hour on a boat, she soon had half of the people as friends. She chatted with everybody, and her gaiety was infectious. She converted several women to Christianity and was very daring in her mixture of affectionate tyranny and eager zeal.

Upper Egypt was very prosperous: gold from eastern Egypt and Ethiopia was traded there, as well as other metals and timber from Ethiopia. The stone quarries were famous, and there were many boat-building yards using the imported timber.

Farming was highly developed on the irrigated land, and food was plentiful. The people there were naturally sociable and friendly, but because of the ease of trade, intellectual activities were not held in high regard. Those successful in business were the local heroes. It was even hard to get the early Christian converts to study. They wanted to accept everything to get it out of the way.

Some of the early converts became great preachers and others could compose popular songs and poems.

Huge Christian rallies became very popular, with preachers moving crowds to tears and laughter. The songs sung by these large gatherings greatly increased the Christian sense of unity and solidarity. There were many generous donations for charitable causes, and large benefactors were respected in the community.

But Karen was concerned at the lack of learning and the strong emphasis on the emotions. What was to stop others who had better singers and preachers from swaying the crowds in a direction different from the Christian Way?

The mutual trust which existed between Christian business men added to their success; and this earned some resentment from outsiders. Some joined the community because of the advantages that membership conferred. This led to a major scandal involving embezzlement of Christian funds by a leading member, that tarnished the image of the community and caused terrible heartache to everyone.

But in spite of everything their numbers grew mightily and there was always a shortage of priests to care for the needs of the faithful. Christian marriages were plentiful, and the number of schools grew rapidly. The Church in Egypt was constant in its demand for more priests to be sent to them from the neighboring Churches.

The general life of ease in the prosperous community made vocations to the priesthood difficult to obtain in the Egyptian region. Karen prayed for vocations and conversions and offered the hardship and worry of her business and the difficulties of her travel for the success of the Christian foundations.

The Roman authorities for the time being were tolerant and regarded Christianity as just another movement within the complexity of their empire. Greek Christian teachers had established themselves in Alexandria.

Joseph carefully rolled the papyrus, placed it back in its copper casket and hung it on the wall of his bedroom.

# CHAPTER 33

## ☙ Ruth

R uth's letter came sometime later.

*"Dearest Father, the treasure of my heart,*

*"I look on your face in my mind's eye as I write this letter and my prayers and many tears come with it.*

*"My heart was overwhelmed when David sent his message that you were alive and that he had been with you. Now that we have communication, thanks to Rome, I shall be writing to you more often. Expense will be the only reason for not writing more.*

*"Our desert group are full of excitement over the prospect of going to the north where they can pray in peace; and many have volunteered to go to Britain. Each one that goes shall be a bearer of a letter from your loving daughter.*

*"Azim died suddenly and had been very active up to the time of his death. I thank the Lord, because a slow and difficult old age would not have suited him.*

*"He died in full vigor and was filled with an active zeal for the ways of the Lord.*

*"Azim did not join the desert Christians, but was very active in their establishment. He led many escaped slaves into the desert,*

*men and women who had proved their loyalty by steadfast service to their new religion.*

*"He seemed to love the fast chariot rides into the desert, taking some new Christian to a new life, remote from the town, the sand spraying in the desert air. He was a genius in getting provisions to them. Many non-slaves have also chosen such a life, and there is great joy among them.*

*"For our part in the towns, the work has been slow. I have given myself to the Lord under the guidance of Mary. The people here are faced with a plethora of gods, some of them not worthy of humans. We work steadily and with patience, waiting on the Lord and doing his will.*

*"I teach Latin for a living, but it is not a popular language here and the people despise it. There are many who speak Greek much better than myself and I would not be able to compete with them in that language. Hebrew is not popular either for historical reasons.*

*"We have many people translating spiritual works into Greek, and we are working to lay good intellectual spiritual foundations for work in the future. We want the intellectual seed of learning to grow intertwined with piety.*

*"I love you and love you, always and always.*

> *"Your daughter,*
> *"Ruth."*

Added to the letter was a long account of her life since Joseph's escape. Ruth had felt the loss of her father more. She was fourteen at the time, while Karen was only nine.

Sometimes she would think, often for the most trivial reasons, that her father was returning, and she would start to prepare for his return.

Gradually, with increasing age, these fantasies declined. She idolized Uncle Reuben, who knew how to tease her intellectual propensities. Ruth was extremely intelligent and loved to spend hours reading.

She would often spend long periods of time chatting to Mary and she would quite cheerfully have died for Mary any time.

When Mary asked whether she would follow the men-folk and go to work among the Parthians, she volunteered immediately.

A group of women set off, led by Azim, who knew the way and would act as interpreter. The men had obtained a house for them, but many of the women found difficulty in getting work. The women of the area tended to marry very young and live in a part of the house set aside for women. The Christian women were not understood, and were despised and avoided by the women of the area.

Ruth's own income was very small, and she quickly learned how to make a little go a long way. The total income of the house was pitifully small.

Azim was upset at the way these celibate women were misunderstood. He would often arrive bringing a basket of fruit, often with sweetmeats as well. He knew that the womenfolk liked sweets.

The men for their part also found the beginnings difficult. The first Christians were from among the slaves, who in general were cruelly treated. Some of the Greek and Jewish slaves were very well educated.

Later it was decided to move from the towns and to become more self-sufficient. Both men and women developed farming skills and learned to weave and make garments. They sold their surplus in order to buy things they could not make for themselves. They kept a strict spiritual regime, no easier than the life of a slave, so no one was tempted to escape from slavery to join them for the wrong reason. The members were carefully chosen only after a long period of testing. Azim would arrange for their escape and none of the other slaves knew of his involvement. He was a master of discretion and noble intrigue.

Martha and Mary visited them sometimes and on one glorious occasion Mary, the mother of Jesus, stayed a long time with them, advising them on the development of their spiritual life, on how to develop a deep spiritual union with her Son through prayer. She recommended her spouse, Joseph, as model for a life of union with her Son. She gave advice on the role of work and prayer in leading a balanced life. Great changes were made in the lives of the groups of both men and women after her visit.

The rigors and worries of the early days took their toll on Ruth, since she had inherited something of her mother's delicate constitution. She was always solicitous for the welfare of the slaves, and sometimes sweetmeats went from Azim's basket straight into the parcels for the slaves, even though the women were short of food themselves. The slaves were unaware of the sacrifices, and sometimes congratulated themselves on having wealthy benefactors.

The number of the faithful grew steadily, and they began to send people to other parts of the Christian world. The desert could only sustain small numbers and even the small amount of food they produced took a great deal of effort. They developed great skill in weaving and painting and in the making of baskets and other wickerwork.

# CHAPTER 34

## ⁓ The Decline

Joseph had five more good years of working energetically until a winter came when he had to spend weeks in bed with breathing difficulties. Although he recovered, he never again had the same zest for life. He smiled more but walked less.

Morvah and Mulfra died within a short time of one another: Morvah quickly, Mulfra slowly, in great pain.

Joseph tended to him day and night. In the evenings before Mulfra slipped into a restless sleep, they would often talk together, watching the flames crackle in the hearth by the bed, their eyes gleaming in the flickering light.

"Joseph, I hope there is music in Heaven. You told me once that some Greeks believe that music lies at the very center of creation. I hope and believe that is true. I was always dissatisfied with my flute playing. It was always too thin an instrument. I wanted my music to soar like a silver bird over mighty oceans or sweeping valleys making dalliance with the wind, but no instruments are heavy or mighty enough to accompany me. Nature itself is too strong. I have tried playing in the open, on the cliff tops and on the mountains, but nature is too strong; my notes blew away like the smoke from a solitary ember in a storm and made no impression."

"You told me, Joseph, that Lucifer is a fallen Cherubim, a prince of music that once entertained the Godhead, until he, with his self-assertive cacophony, rebelled against the harmony of creation. Did the Archangel Michael and sweet Jesus restore harmony to broken creation, to death and suffering, by giving it meaning?

"Suffering is such a mystery. I cannot comprehend it. I dislike pain; and death I fear. How has God harmonized it with his goodness? Has death and suffering been interwoven with a higher music, which is beyond our ken and which has blunted the barbs of our iniquity?

"If this is not true, then life is indeed incomprehensible and meaningless. Assure me, Joseph, I feel so uncertain."

"Mulfra, my dear friend," whispered Joseph. "I saw such pain as you would not believe. Not just physical pain, but the intense, intense suffering of rejection. I saw the man bear the sordid sins of the world; a man who, as God, saw them in all their detail of selfishness and hatred. Yet, I did not see despair. I saw intense love with all the burning desire to atone and fulfill the wishes of his Father, God. To the last detail.

"I did not see despair or doubt. I saw the cross triumph in that mighty shout: 'My God, my God, why hast thou forsaken me?' the opening lines of one of the mightiest psalms in all the psalms of David. And do you know the closing line of that psalm, Mulfra?

'I too shall live on in his presence,
and beget children to serve him;
these to a later age shall speak of the Lord's name;
these to a race that must yet be born
shall tell the story of his faithfulness,
hear what the Lord did.'" (Ps 22 [21] Douai)

"For these past months, Joseph, I have been marching to the throbbing beat of my pain, like to a drum calling me to a great gathering. In my prayer I heard sweet refrains of music, finely practiced, which gave me an indication that the calling is not wrathful. The beat and the pain has been getting louder lately. I do not have much further to travel.

"Maybe, when I reach the clearing in this forest of my final journey, I shall be invited to sit with the Cherubim to make witty and harmonious music, cleverly rhythmic to instruments of God's creating. What a merry sound we shall make!"

Joseph was there on the final day.

He knelt by Mulfra's bed during the final agony. He saw a look of indescribable affection enter into the eyes of Mulfra.

Just before he died, Mulfra gave a little wave; maybe he saw another, finer audience as he played out the last act of the drama, which was for real.

Joseph heard the death rattle and saw the tear streak its way down Mulfra's cheek, a sign of his final dissolution, a little rivulet, like the water from the side of Jesus on the cross.

"Well done! Mulfra," something which he had often said to him, after one of their little theater pieces.

Joseph closed the curtains of his eyes and for the first time ever, kissed the forehead; the salt of the sweat tasted on his lips, but it was as nothing compared to the salt and vinegar, which was pickling his entrails in the barrel of his body.

He took a small handkerchief and wiped away the tear. Joseph was to keep it for several weeks, during the Eucharist, as a reminder.

Mulfra had died offering his suffering for his sins and those of others, and the twinkling humor in his eyes never left, even in his final agony.

It probably was the exertions of these visits and the physical loss of Mulfra's friendship and company, which brought on Joseph's own illness.

A winter came when he spent weeks in bed, breathing with difficulty. A fire burned continuously in his house day and night, and his care came under the direction of Eleanor and her helpers.

Although he recovered, he never had the same zest for life.

Slowly, the trained Christians from Corinth trickled back to Britain and entered into the labor. Days became filled with a regular routine.

The hermits made big inroads into the countryside, many British joining them.

They worked a great deal in stone, and brought new ways of farming, particularly in sheep-raising. They introduced weaving and dyeing of wool, searching out new colors from plants and lichens.

Their fencing for the animal pens was stone and such walls gave a great air of permanence and settlement. Local people copied their ways, and even their forms of prayer became familiar to them.

With the growth of Greek and Roman learning, the works of Joseph fell into decline. His theaters pieces were too primitive for the younger folk since they were more interested in the modern ways of the Romans.

Mulfra's and Joseph's plays became things of nostalgia for the old folk.

New learning in Greek and Roman and the letters of the saints replaced the learning of Joseph. The disciples of Joseph had become much more learned than the master, and his advice became something to be tolerated patiently rather than to be followed.

On occasion they would still invite him to speak about the early days, and his speeches were accepted with politeness. Things were now done with more time and in less of a hurry, with much less improvisation, particularly in regard to the Sacraments.

Joseph was no longer in the center of things and he devoted more of his days to prayer, content that after his death the work would continue.

As he walked with increasing difficulty, the locals made him a little donkey cart covered with canvass, with a bronze bowl inside that burned charcoal to keep him warm on the cold days. He often drove his little donkey, sometimes accompanied by Eleanor, to the cliff top and looked west over the sea.

" Eleanor?, I am troubled."

"And why?"

"In Heaven, I don't know who should fill my heart more, my wife, Rebecca, or you. I think I shall have to put you at opposite ends of Heaven and visit you both at the same time." Joseph's eyes twinkled.

"Joseph, you sound like a bigamist, you silly sentimental old man. Look towards the sun hidden behind those clouds. The only way one sunbeam can communicate with another is to go back to its source, the sun, and then down to the other. Our hearts shall be totally filled with Jesus; and all love shall be by him, with him and through him. We shall all love one another as one, with the one total and entire Jesus Love."

"Thou hast spoken well, oh Christian," said Joseph in mock reverence. "If we had married so many years ago, I would have indeed been a bigamist, not knowing that my wife was alive . . .

"With your lineage, Eleanor, we could have had children with red, brown, black, yellow or white hair. . . . Look what a unity of Christian nations that would have presented to the world. . . . In our tribe, hair is always black. Red hair is unknown. . . . When I first saw you, I thought your head was on fire. Instead, the flames came out of your mouth. I thought you were going to consume me with fire."

Eleanor changed the subject gently, musing slowly and half speaking to herself, trying to pick the words carefully.

"It was you that brought the fire, and it has enkindled the fire of many of our people. . . . Maybe your fire is more gentle . . . and I think it has subdued mine from an outer fire to an inner one.

"God is good! . . .

"If you had not come, I probably would have ended my days being pushed around a palace floor, old like a cleaning rag. Now each of us are busily preparing for a new beginning. Our cleaning rags are busy in our interior household, removing the stains and polishing the dwelling, so that it is more suitable for the Trinity to dwell in.

"Oh, the gentle fire of the Holy Spirit. This hearth fire of ours gives us comfort, light for our intellect and warmth for our will. My father was right when he said that Christ's love has ended the futility of our days and given us life's purpose. Always a new beginning, a new simplicity.

"All that matters is to keep our hearth fire burning and our house in order, so that we give light and heat to others and show them that our dwelling is delightful. This is our purpose, and . . . the reason of our being. Christ's coming has shown that to us.

"We seek the end, by preparing a beginning, and continue to rekindle our hearts from the fire of God's love until they are eventually consumed by that love."

Joseph looked at Eleanor.

"Eleanor, there is no describing the bitterness I held in my heart when I came to Britain. . . . When I was humiliated by the Romans I lay gasping, biting my tongue with a burning hatred. The anger came out of me like a giant wave, suddenly rising out of a calm sea and roaring down on me, pressing me down in its raging fury.

"Christ had appeared to me, had shown me his love before ascending to His Father in Heaven; but it was just words to me.

"I suppressed the anger, as well as I could . . . by trying to forget; but events continued to remind me, and my insides would become like a raging furnace. I wanted to breath fire, burning up those around me and striking my opponents with fierce claws. I was the hidden dragon . . .

"But the good God spared me from excess. Without him, I am sure I would have ended my days violently and with great bitterness . . .

"Futility is the gaping wound everywhere; and I would have ended my days in violent revolution, seeking as with an opiate to dull the pain of my existence. Worse, because of my innate cowardice, I would have drowned myself in sin, so that in self indulgence I would have sought to delay the vision of my own ineptitude.

"The worst elements I have seen, Eleanor, are those revolutionaries, who are gross in their immorality. Among them the devil makes his lair. When they go to battle, Satan rides with them.

"They recruit by corruption, and gradually train themselves in the art of hatred. I watched these men—extreme violence in their action—driven by suicidal despair. If Satan was with them, then what interest had he in the new Israel wrought by violence? Is this the way that God wants the establishment of the new kingdom?

"It was then . . . before Christ, that I began to have doubts about the righteousness of our methods. . . . Can the new Kingdom be wrought by violence? Of what import is territory?

"Is this the design of Satan to convert the covenant of Israel into idolatry? Is this why he has such a desire to establish the Kingdom of Israel by violence?

"Eleanor; I, unwittingly, was working for him.

"Christ has brought a new covenant to Israel the covenant of personal love; and only Christ can bring personal love. Oh how the good Lord led me gently through the swamps of my passion, and the violence of the storm until he fed me with his own Body.

"My soul did not feel at peace until I had brought him into my home. He cleaned me, when I could not. A dirty rag cannot clean anything. He extinguished the fires in the fabric of my house and left one burning in the hearth of my being.

"Eleanor, a crucifixion is terrible. I hope you never see one. I stood by Caiphas on Calvary. All of us shuddered at each breath that Christ took on the cross; as he struggled to raise his body on the nails, in order to breathe. It is a miracle that Mary did not die there and then.

"I saw the loving eyes of Jesus look at us without trace of hatred or malice. . . . 'My God, my God, why hast thou forsaken me?' he said with the measured rhythm of the psalm . . . and he looked at us. I heard Caiphas gasp: 'Even now he is quoting from the scriptures.'

"What unfathomable depths of love could make a man give his last sentence on earth to his executioner?

"I pray that Caiphas, in the quiet moments of reflection, was converted, and that now he is kissing the five wounds of Christ in heaven as I would like to do when I die. What heart can be so hard and remain unmoved by such a death?

"The fires of hatred cannot be extinguished by ourselves, because the conflagration is too great. Truly, I can say it is not I that loves, but him that dwells in me.

"The New Israel shall be established like the whispering of air that nourishes the garden and makes all things sweet to the senses. The new kingdom shall be a garden . . . not a fortress. A new Garden of Eden.

"That is where I was so terribly mistaken, Eleanor; in my vanity and stupidity I thought the New Israel would be wrought by violence and conquest. I thought I should be a warrior, when I should have been a gardener, tending the gentle shoots of our young generation, giving them the qualities desired by the Almighty. Leave power and glory to His Majesty who can bring down the mighty of this earth in the twinkling of an eye. From us he desires gentleness, humility and constancy as his beloved Son has taught us."

Joseph turned. "A strange thing, Eleanor: you know how much I like to come here to pray; yet, I find it much easier to pray facing west than facing east, the direction of our Lord's birthplace. . . . It is as though our Blessed Lord wants me to pray in this direction. . . . It is as though he is trying to tell me, that this place is not the edge of the world, but the center. Christ has only drawn half a circle, and maybe he wants to complete the orb, using our land as the pivot."

CHAPTER 35

# ⚜ The Closing
# of the Day

Things did not go smoothly in the shires of western Britain. Conversions were made among the Belgae and tribes from the East; and some of these sought shelter from Roman wrath by moving into the Christian community of the British in the west. It took a great deal of effort on Joseph's part to prevent friction.

He seemed to anticipate trouble and was always at hand steering feelings away from strife and into the calmer waters of quiet diplomacy. Many sermons were on the topic of peace, and there was always fear that discord would enter into the community.

The Romans still sought the western British as allies and that spared them the persecutions and reprisals occurring in the east.

Joseph was always worried that some incident would spark Roman anger and bring a terrible split among the Roman Christians, the British, and the Belgians and easterners.

On top of these worries came another. Among the second-generation Christians, there came an increasing attraction to the ways of Rome. Its might, power, administration, and order impressed them. They were familiar with Christianity and had never known life without a Redeemer. They took Christian life for granted.

They found the pomp and ceremony given to pagan gods artistically interesting and found the Roman separation between religion and morals convenient.

Joseph had seen many Romanizing Jews in his youth. The superficiality of their learning caused him to despise them, but because of them he had studied the law and the prophets deeply.

He argued with them but got nowhere.

The reason, he reflected as he grew older, was not because of the intellectual weakness of the religion of their fathers, but because it was morally demanding.

He saw the same desires in poor people and those of poor education seeking to climb the stairway of social prestige, not by the central staircase of their own merit, but by the back stairs that lead to the bedrooms.

These people affect airs and graces and poise but their lives are empty.

Joseph smelled this odor, like that of a putrid animal rotting in some hidden corner of a building.

The Roman baths and amphitheatres were exciting places for the wealthier young Christians, while the ways of the British seemed dull and hard.

Piety was boring. Religion was practiced in a desultory manner, mostly to please their parents, but with little enthusiasm.

Joseph was old, and his lack of energy and tiredness prevented him from reaching them.

They tolerated him but with a certain degree of discomfort. They felt happier when he was not there. Their conversation could relax then, and they needn't be on their guard.

Joseph spent many days and long evenings locked in prayer over these insidious developments. He felt so powerless.

A particular concern was a former pupil of his. A boy from a very poor background whose education he had subsidized. He had high intelligence, but, possibly as a result of the humiliations he had suffered because of his poverty, he had a burning ambition for success and fame.

His name was Fride, a British name, but he altered it to Phaedus, almost the same as Phaedrus, but not quite; he chose to imply, but not exactly to assume the mantle of that freedman of Augustus and pupil of Socrates, a well-known writer of Roman fables.

Similarly, he painted his leather shoes, but not in the colors of the Roman officials' lest he attract their ire.

His Roman clothes were precise, but he wore them awkwardly, since he had not grown up wearing them naturally. His Roman was good, but he had a slight British accent that the Roman women found attractive.

His body was thickset from hard work as a youth but even this combined with a slight coarseness was earthily attractive to Roman women, especially those brought up in the indolent, soft comfort of wealthy Roman households.

The men of these households tended to be soft, affected, and effete. Phaedus was still tough, and had rugged good looks.

He had two Roman women as lovers, wives of wealthy Roman merchants, and each in her vanity thought that she was the sole object of his attention.

"If he doesn't find a rich Roman widow soon, he is heading for poverty and disaster," thought Joseph.

High living, and no income, with mounting debts: already his middle was showing the effects of overeating and lack of exercise, and a double chin was beginning to appear.

Later on balding might become a problem. It was looked on with disfavor by Romans.

In the meantime Joseph was afraid of the damage Phaedus might do to his Christian community. He was becoming a noted wit and satirist and he ridiculed Christian asceticism. He had a great following among the young.

He also wrote a book on "Ethics"—a mixture of Greek and Roman etiquette with a few earthy wisdoms from British culture.

It was too superficial to affect metanoia or change of heart, but because it was so easily understandable, it met with instant success among those who wished to philosophize but did not care for the mental effort and study required. It formed a good conversation piece for dinners and informal gatherings.

A particular object of his satirical works were the hermits in the mountains, but of course they were too far removed from the orbit of Roman society to be directly affected.

They recruited from the remote villages and towns with difficult access. Occasionally members of local wealthy families, well-educated, would go and join them. Satire and ridicule had aroused their curiosity, and they became inspired by the simplicity of the hermits' life and their intense knowledge of Greek, Roman, and Hebrew learning. Many of these hermits had made it their life's work to preserve and translate the best writings of the three cultures, as support for a Christian culture.

Joseph worried more and more about the intellectual safety of his flock. His way of learning was hard and disciplined and here was someone offering a way which was witty, easy to understand, and deceptively simple.

"Without Me you cannot," the phrase came drifting into Joseph's head as he prayed.

"Oh Lord, please give us weapons to fight this contagion."

Joseph prayed and prayed and fasted. He tried fasting without food, but it made him weak and ill; and so he tried the fasting of his will by not giving in to his desires for laziness and comfort, and sought the fasting of his intellect by more intense study, even though he found his memory and concentration increasingly difficult.

"Oh Lord, give us weapons." The Lord seemed not to answer him.

Joseph almost began to despair, but one day in his despondency he remembered the words of Mary.

"Because of you this land shall receive more graces and blessings than the rain."

"Sweet Lady, purest of Virgins, please dedicate this land, as your dowry, to our Heavenly Father.

"Give it purity and strength of character that it may resist the insidious snares of Lucifer.

"Send us St. Michael the Archangel to defend our land."

# CHAPTER 36

## ❧ The Counterattack

"What these young people need is sport, games, competition, hikes, and the companionship that adventure brings with it."

These were the words of a red-faced Roman Christian soldier, Artemus, as he and Joseph looked at a group of young men idling their time away, near a fountain, with no real purpose.

"In the army, if you let laziness creep in, you can expect endless trouble.

"Keep 'em busy. And they will fight for you. If you neglect them or leave them unoccupied, they get self-indulgent and cowardly. It's a sure recipe for getting killed."

Joseph was struck by the words. He paused, looked at Artemus, then stared at the group of youngsters, patted Artemus on the back and hurried to his house.

He had writing to do and plans to make.

From that day, Joseph started his youth drive. He first informed the older Christians of his plans, to seek their support for his efforts together with their prayers. He then formulated his plans.

From parents and young men, faithful to the Faith, he demanded action.

"I want groups for music and drama . . .

"I want sport, lots of it, competitions, prizes, honors . . . strength. "Oh Azim, please help them," he thought to himself.

"I want camps, excursions, fishing, hunting.

Ladies, I want the girls to be taught how to properly keep and decorate their homes, inside and out, how to make nice clothes, to play instruments and do handicrafts, to sing and dance in a refined and elegant way, to prepare new and attractive dishes. They also need excursions and competitions of their own.

We will overcome evil by drowning it in goodness. We shall not fear the world nor its allurements, but use it for God's purposes. We have forgotten, in our troubles, that the blessed Lord has a sense of humor. We have become too heavyhearted.

"We must love the Lord in times of woe and we must love the Lord in times of ease and plenty . . .

"Each has its season.

"Each is a new song to the Lord.

"Laughter and merriment shall mix with our tears. It is not only the sad saints that enter heaven, but the happy ones much more so."

And so it came to pass. Joseph worked with fury, recruiting, persuading, encouraging, inspiring the idealistic, encouraging the doubtful, and above all seeking out the ones with ability to organize.

The most successful groups were the ones who prayed the most and followed their words with concrete action, done with originality and initiative.

"You must be saturated in prayer, like bread soaked in wine." Joseph was speaking to the leaders of the young.

"The young must respect you because of your personal qualities.

"We have to give them the necessary human qualities, like the virtues of the Romans—courage, resourcefulness, loyalty, generosity, toughness, ability to organize, broadmindedness, leadership.

"Those virtues represent the wisdom and the effort of man, and we must not waste the order of things, our nature as humans, made by God.

"We perfect them by the light of reason . . .

"To this clay we must 'breath in' the Divine.

"I repeat, you must be people of piety: you must quench your thirst at the fountains of the Sacraments; you receive from them the grace and strength, like fuel on the fire.

"The young will respect your integrity of life.

"By your friendship and care, you must earn their respect and, when they ask, tell them of the higher things of God. We know that these alone will alloy the base metal of their hearts with the gold and silver of Divine Love, the gifts and fruits of the Holy Spirit . . . charity, joy, peace, patience, goodness and delicate and refined kindness.

"Give them ideals. Things to hope for in the shaping of their personality . . .

"Give them joy and good humor. If possible do not scold them, but point to them the better things.

"Lead them by kindness.

"Expose what is false by wit and irony. Satan hates the witty and good humored. Lead them gently to a life of piety and a life of study and noble work.

"To develop the intellect and the will is the way to eternal youth and optimism. Only these faculties of the soul are not subject to decay; they lead us to eternal youth and to eternal joy. 'I will go unto the altar of God for he giveth joy to my youth,' as the Psalms tell us.

"Oh parents! What a task you have in the upbringing of your little ones!

"Tell them stories where truth and beauty triumph and in this way build up their sense of right and wrong. Telling them such stories is like pressing beautiful images into wax.

"Give them, by these tales, nobleness of character. Later on when they find that life is more complicated, they will still carry the imprint of these simple ideals and these will guide them. Life is a struggle for simplicity. Let us hold on to it in spite of the subtle traps laid for us on our path. Truth and goodness are simple; evil is contorted and complicated. The devil is the father of all lies.

"Tell them stories from the Old Testament, of the heroes of Israel, simply and with meaning. Tell them about the life of Jesus and the fulfillment of the promises of God. Above all be a friend and counselor to your children; do not be too heavy or distant from them. Later on in their youth they will trust you as a faithful and trusted advisor; one of experience, whose opinion is valued. Even if at first, in their youthful arrogance, they think they have all the answers, nature and its savage cruelty will drive them back to you, provided you have not closed your door to them. Be patient and trust in the ways of the Lord, who can make all crooked paths straight.

"And in those magic moments when your children want to fight or play with you, when they want to take you to their toy house or hill fort, go with them; enter their world, and do not through selfishness leave them alone while pursuing your own selfish comforts. These are moments for the building of great friendship and confidence that will enable you to weather the difficult times when they are in need of strong correction. Hold them with the bonds of affection and the fear that they will lose your respect. Always trust them even though at times through weakness they have betrayed that trust. In those moments remember your own worst weaknesses, and it will help you to be more understanding.

"And yet, parents, knowledge of the ways of the Lord, personal friendship, and mutual respect, though important, are not the most important. We have to train them to personal virtue; that strength of character needed to stand up to the snares and temptations of this life. From an early age we must teach them to be generous and to live for others, gently, according to their capacity. Teach them first to be kind and considerate to their brothers and sisters and playmates; ease them out of grasping for themselves alone. As they get older, educate them to be concerned about wider issues; the problems of the sick and the poor. Give them sympathy for those who are unfortunate in our society. Show them how to be polite and respectful and to adjust their behavior according to whom they are with. Show them how to be polite and to give outward signs of love and respect.

"Watch the company they keep. Be very strict if you see them getting into bad company. The change in their character is almost immediately recognized if you are solicitous in their care. Seek out good companions for them, before they themselves find bad ones. Let them join groups who are wholesome and merry and have a healthy piety. Give them sound advice and then the freedom to develop their own way in life.

"In childhood show them the virtue of work. Do not be over-indulgent with them. Let them realize how much effort it takes to earn the things they want to have. Do not train them into the mentality that whatever they want they can get, since this breeds laziness and resentment.

"You, dear parents know how to do these things better than I. You know your own children and how to accomplish these things according to their temperament. Each virtue must be put in place with love and kisses according to your own fashioning. This is a grace you receive in matrimony. Do it as well as you can, asking the Holy Family of Nazareth to be your guides and helpers.

"If, in spite of everything humanly possible, they stray, because they have free will, entrust them to Jesus and Mary and do not judge. It is not for us to judge, but to love and understand. Try in your anger and hurt not to close the door on them, but always try to ensure that they can return without too much loss of face. Be patient—yours is the work of a lifetime. You may have to wait sometimes until the coming of grandchildren, before you begin to see the fruits of your work. Always be happy in trying your best, God can do the rest."

# CHAPTER 37

## ☙ Cutting the Cord

Eleanor in the meantime was having troubles of her own. The society of women she had started for alleviation of the sufferings of slaves and the care of the neglected and abandoned, had grown.

Her work at the school had meant that she could not care for this society as she would like; and like any good administrator, she had chosen someone to take this task from her shoulders.

She had chosen a woman of piety and common sense, reasonably intelligent and with a spirit of initiative, This woman inspired her followers by the loving care she gave them.

Fortunately, or unfortunately, she also had a very strong will. Her plans did not always agree with Eleanor's. She was a vigorous organizer and was never idle.

Their meetings became painful affairs. They would walk around each other like stag-beetles, fearful lest they might lock their horns together in combat and fearful of the scandal they would cause if they were to quarrel. Long silences used to ensue, when they would each struggle for charity.

"Ana, the ladies must pray more, they need more spiritual sustenance if they are to endure."

"I think their present piety is enough. I don't want ladies who go into escapist dream worlds. I want strong women who are prepared to get their hands dirty and not avoid their duties by pious conversation," replied Ana. "My . . . I mean our ladies must be women who can make practical prayer out of their daily duties. Prayer can be a subtle form of escapism, avoiding the difficult, to go into a dream world."

"That is not true prayer, Ana," replied Eleanor quietly. "True prayer is a struggle to see the will of God in our every action. We struggle to see as God sees, to find the Will of God for ourselves through prayer every day. And, above all, to beg and beg our Lord to help us overcome our miseries, and to have the strength to carry on. We must learn to love, to really love—unselfish love—and we must learn to give God due honor and praise.

"Only in this way can our actions be purposeful and bear fruit. We must avoid the danger of thoughtless action, which is the fruit of our own will . . . not God's."

"But, Eleanor, you are so boring with this endless pious talk. What about the prayer of action, the prayer of actually doing good, not talking. Anyone can talk piously."

"Oh, Ana. What is our real purpose here on earth? It is not to establish fine works and enterprises. God can do that in an instant. We are here to converse with Christ in the little moments of everyday even in the midst of our work.

"This is our real life's work, Ana. Our human ambitions are only a means, not an end.

"The fruit of our effort must be love, real love. It is a necessary forerunner to Divine Love. Our companions must learn daily acts of self-denial if they are to remain united in love. Otherwise our enterprise will fail in disunity.

"Seek real Love. And you will see everything in its proper place, in the right order of things. The ambition of Jesus for us is far greater than anything we can achieve on our own merits. It can only be wrought by prayer, by grace, and a willing obedience to the Will of God.

"When we feel bored, it is Christ gently calling us to his Cross. He is calling us away from what is sensible to what is valiant. He is calling us to virtue.

"We must seek virtue primarily, not human ambition, virtues derived from the sacraments, supernatural virtues, which are placed in our heart by the Divine Master himself.

"Even if, at the end of our days, Ana, our temple of prayer and virtue only looks like a child's toy or a foolish ruin, then God, who sees the love that we have put into our efforts, will not be displeased, because '*Amor vincit omnia*' Love conquers all."

"What we must do, Ana, is see Christ in those we care for and for that we must be like him, through prayer, Ana, through prayer."

"I am sure God will help us as we go along." Ana replied, cutting short the conversation and going back to her work.

Eleanor held her head, placed her hands on her cheeks and struggled to hold back her tears. She knew that this state of affairs could not endure.

She prayed and prayed and then consulted Joseph.

"Ana has a good heart and you cannot best her, Eleanor, in energy and organization, and she is confident, although a bit too confident.

"There will be defections, because the ladies are not receiving the sustenance for the long arid days when we live only by faith, hope . . . and a love that seems remote. But do not fret yourself, Eleanor. We are slow learners, and are slow to realize what we need, in personal qualities, for the task given to us.

"Jesus is patient with us, his children, and tolerant of our mistakes and defects. He realizes how incompetent we are and smiles at our follies. He knows full well that we want to love him in spite of all our stupidities. Eventually, God will complete his plans, in spite of us.

"He allows us to interfere and mess up his plans because he loves us. What loving father stops a child from helping him in the garden even though the toddler keeps falling on the plants he is supposed to be tending. Do not lose your joy or your peace, Eleanor; to do so is pride. Pride in thinking we are competent.

"Write to her, Eleanor from a distance. Add what is missing and leave the rest to God. Ana has chosen to live by experience, then it is by experience that she will learn."

It was agreed that Eleanor was to leave the Association in order to maintain unity and avoid a split in the organization: to sever links and to allow the Association to drift free. She would write letters to Ana.

This severance cut into Eleanor's flesh deeply. The ladies loved and respected her, their affection was a source of consolation. Now she would leave and give them their freedom, and there would not be even an occasional visit. She would pray for them and love them from a distance. Emotionally she had come to depend on their affection.

Now she was alone again.

"You don't tolerate rivals, do you Lord?" she grimaced in her prayer. "I have never met such a possessive person in my whole life," she continued.

"No wonder they crucified you, since you seem to go around crucifying everybody else."

Gradually Eleanor calmed down.

"I love you, Jesus, very much. I remember when, over the body of my husband, I thought of taking poison.

"I prayed to the God of Israel to help me in my suffering and I seemed to hear the words 'Be patient and wait.'

"I waited, keeping at bay my husband's relatives, using my wits and my tongue to hold back their plots and their schemes over my husband's possessions, playing one group against another and never daring to share my anxieties with anyone for fear that my revelations would give my enemies advantage. I roared like a lion, but my heart was as fearful as a lamb.

"When I felt the urge to go down to the village and saw the stranger by the pool, I knew he was a Jew even before he started washing.

"I knew he had a message for me. I wanted to wring it from him. But, be calm: be patient and wait: and the final eternity of a wait until he came to me at my home. Be calm: be patient and wait. If he has come this far, then God can surely send him the short distance up the hill!

"How true! How slowly and carefully you revealed the message to me at a pace at which I could understand. A message revealed in word, in drama, and the slow experience of living and learning. How patient you are with us dumb creatures!

"But now, dear Jesus. You seem to have destroyed my life's work.

"I am alone. A person cannot live without love, and you have taken away all my loved ones. I seem to have no one to love.

"If you had wanted us to love like angels you would have made us as such. You made us human, and humans fear to be alone. Send your angels to comfort me. The ascending angels to carry me to you in prayer, and the descending angels to bring me your grace and help.

"Oh what agony you must have suffered in the garden of Gethsemane! I can hardly bear this small slight. How could you bear the vision of the sins of the world in all their sordid detail and rest this divine knowledge on your human frame, the mortal frame of thy body? Thy loneliness there makes my loneliness here seem trivial. Oh help me, Jesus. I do not have thy strength. I am so sad that I find it hard to breathe."

"You are not alone. You have one other," came the idea floating into the bowed head of Eleanor.

"Joseph."

## The Parting of the Ways

"I have given the monks a list of broths, so that you don't get a repeat of that chest complaint. And they are to light a fire if they see that the cold is getting you down."

Both Eleanor and Joseph had sold all their possessions and given the money to the various needy of the area and also to their beloved school.

They had already given money to the two communities entrusted to their care in old age. The women's community of ladies sent by Ruth and dedicated to prayer had been established in the kingdom of Chun.

Joseph's abode was in the west, facing the sea, separated by the mountains from the land of Chun.

"See you in heaven, Eleanor!"

"Take care of yourself, Joseph. Wool is very warm, if you cover it on the outside with leather to keep out the wind. And wear heavy boots. Cold can enter the body through the feet."

Their two little carts parted, as they left the crowd, which had gathered to say their farewell.

They were never to meet again.

# CHAPTER 38

## ❧ Joseph's Days

Joseph's journey took many days; his little donkey cart and his escort made steady progress over the hill tracks and valleys, sometimes camping, sometimes staying at the houses of friends made in the vigorous days of his journeys into the interior.

Most of the farewells were tearful as families pressed him to stay longer. Little presents were dropped into his cart as he left, by friends who realized that they would probably not see him again.

Joseph had reached the stage where he showed little outward emotional reaction. Looking at them steadily, he promising them his prayers and intercessions.

The channel was almost perfectly calm when the cart and donkey and passengers were rowed across into the land of the Silurians. Then he slowly journeyed west hugging the channel coast.

The brethren came out to meet him and led him to his stone house, overlooking the sea as Eleanor had directed. They had built it especially for him. There was a fire burning in the fireplace.

There Joseph spent his days, reading, until his eyes failed him; writing for a little longer, until that too became impossible; and collecting plants that seemed similar by their smell to the herbs that Azim had pointed out to him as being medicinal. Stylas who had practiced medicine in the East joined him in his task, writing down descriptions of the plants and their usefulness. They collected dried herbs in jars for later infusions.

Joseph liked Stylas, his calmness and his quiet gentle manner. Joseph still struggled to rise early with the rest of the brethren. Someone was delegated to check whether Joseph was fit to rise with them each morning. The food was altered to cope with his digestion.

A broad belt was fitted round his waist during the day so someone could help keep him from falling when walking over rough ground. He now stayed in the compound and seldom ventured out. He had long since stopped going on solitary retreats or days of recollection, living alone in the beehive-shaped stone cells on the mountainsides. He used to love those days, talking alone with God as he watched the roll of mist-like rain sweeping the valley below or listening to the rain pattering on the bracken, as he snuggled deeper into the dry hay of the cell.

Letters to his children and friends were no longer possible but periodic news bulletins were dispatched.

Years passed in the slow rhythmic cycle of life in the compound.

The end was relatively brief. That evening had found Joseph more tired than usual and there was a deep ache inside his chest cavity. His ankles had been swelling and he needed extra pillows in order to sleep. He felt a reluctance to go to bed and sat on a chair by the doorway after Stylas had left him. He looked to the shadows of the hills. Spring was beginning to appear and all the hillsides were beginning to burst alive with freshness and bright color. The afternoon had been very bright, after a brisk morning shower, and all the leaves had danced in sunlight. The sight had cheered Joseph. Now he sat in the chair to accommodate his ache as best he could.

"I am dying, Jesus. Make my coming to thee be swift; when I have to render account to thee of my life, I am afraid. I have lived a self-centered life. Yet lonely people, O Lord, tend to be self-centered. It's so hard to forget oneself and fill one's life with the

needs of others when one is an alien in a foreign land. Forgive me,
Lord for my excuses.

"O Great God, you appointed Joseph, to be the spouse and
protector for the chastity of Mary.

"For me, you picked Eleanor.

"How tough and unsentimental she has been with me and yet
how much she anticipated my needs even before I realized them
myself. Was the hidden hand of Mary acting through her?

"Even now Eleanor writes to the head of the group here, to
give instructions and commands for my welfare, in order to soften
the rough ways of men. What is this, but the hand of Mary?

"What fool said that women were the weaker sex? They are
much stronger than men. Eleanor was swifter than an Irish
hound in protecting me from life's temptations, snapping and
snarling. I am sure she could have brought down a hind in one
bite, and oh how I used to tease her!

"Look after her final days, Lord, that they be filled with peace
and tranquility."

Joseph watched the clouds pass swiftly over the moon in the
night breeze, like silvery ice floes in a thawing river.

The moon was full and clear.

Joseph passed the night watching the pale light. He watched
the mountain grow lighter with the dawn and listened to the
dawn chorus. "Oh, why do so many people miss the dawn? How
beautiful it is! How easy it is to pray to God in dawn's early light!"

The sun broke through between a gap in the mountains and
shone in Joseph's face. Joseph sank to his knees in the doorway.

Stylas hurried to Joseph's house in the early morning since
he had noticed a slight change in Joseph's attitude the previous
evening. He had looked longer at him in the evening light as he
said goodnight and had taken longer to say his farewell than usual.

When Stylas arrived he found Joseph on his knees slumped
against the door of the house looking inland. By the way his
arms were crumpled he was apparently suffering severe chest
pains. His eyes were fixed on the cross erected by the brethren on
the nearby hill.

"I am sorry, Lord, I am not able to die as you died. I never had your strength.

"Forgive me, Lord; the times when I have put down my little cross, when I ought not have done any such thing.

"Look with compassion on my mediocre life, a life filled with little things that I have tried to do for you."

Stylas cupped his hand behind Joseph's neck and sweeping his other arm under his legs carried him to the bed. Joseph had become very light in weight.

"I don't want to lie down!" cried Joseph. "I have still not conquered the fear of death."

"That is not within your gift, but comes from God above," replied Stylas. "Imagine you are on a cart going to meet your Redeemer, who is waiting for you."

"Not a cart, not a cart. A donkey, a donkey," whispered Joseph.

Stylas placed him on the bed, but before releasing his hand from behind his neck, he arranged the pillows to give Joseph's head some height. He realized that part of Joseph's fear was in lying flat and thereby finding it difficult to breathe. He wanted to remove the hairshirt that he wore, next to his skin, but Joseph forbade him.

The brethren began to intone the "Song of Solomon"—in Hebrew, to respect Joseph's wish that the language of his fathers and his fathers' fathers should be in his ears at the moment of his passing from this life to the next.

> I slept, but my heart was awake
> Hark! My beloved is knocking.
> Open to me, my sister, my love,
> my dove, my perfect one,
> for my head is wet with dew,
> my locks with the drops of the night.
> I had put off my garment,
> How could I put it on?
> I had bathed my feet,

How could I soil them?
My beloved put his hand to the latch,
and my heart was thrilled within me.

Joseph smiled at Stylas as slowly the donkey quickened it's pace; Joseph was growing younger with each step, until he leaped from his mount with a mighty leap, his limbs and body bearing marks of the five wounds of his Saviour, to greet his Rebecca, Reuben, and Ruth and the joyful throng of British who had gone before him.

# CHAPTER 39

## ✣ The Days of Eleanor

As Eleanor bade farewell to the ladies, Blonwen stood like a confused little girl at the end of the pathway. Since her husband's death, Blonwen had helped the ladies considerably in the care of slaves.

"Oh how charity gives such youthfulness to the soul," thought Eleanor as she went to greet her.

"Dear Blonwen. It is a miracle that love and kindliness has preserved her in such simplicity."

Blonwen first held Eleanor's hands, and then put one hand behind Eleanor's back and with the palm of the other hand against Eleanor's cheek pressed Eleanor's head to her shoulder. She cradled her for a while and then drew back and said,

"Who will guide me when you are gone?"

"You are to be the guide, Blonwen. With that kind heart of yours shower your children and your grandchildren, like April rain, so that like little shoots they grow strong and healthy under your attention."

Eleanor's smile began to quiver at the corners. Blonwen showed no such inhibition, and tears came out in thick drops as though from a deep wound.

Eleanor's journey to the land of the Chun was easier, part of the way passing along roads prepared by Roman engineers. She was returning to her kinsfolk and relatives, some now in the second and third generation.

The ladies of dedicated life came out to greet her on arrival and led her into a room where refreshments had been prettily prepared, and the room was scented with flowers. Aromatic herbs lay in bowls near the window-light, and a fire crackled in the fireplace to air the room even though it was summer.

Thus, Eleanor spent her days.

Eleanor had a strong mind and kept her faculties until the very end. Her relatives constantly visited her to ask for her prayers and advice.

Many a husband waited apprehensively for a returned wife armed with authority from "on high," muttering thus:

> "Why is it that women only use rules when it suits them and, when they are clearly in the wrong, the argument turns on whether you like them or not? Men usually are not fast enough to catch the change.
>
> "Why can't priest advisors train men to be more fierce and emotionally ruthless like the womenfolk? Grin and bear it and offer it up is all they offer us menfolk.
>
> "And the most ruthless ploy of all—affection: feminine hands tugging the side burns, nose to nose, eye to eye, forehead to forehead and then the kiss and the hug: to protest would mean being a cad.
>
> "It's a good thing I've got my chums and we can toss a stone in the ring together. A quiet game and calm understanding.
>
> "It's the lot of men to be bullied."

Eleanor had a large discrete influence in the land of the Chun. She was always extremely busy, either writing or working in the garden—which was her delight. After Joseph's death she told many stories about incidents in the life of Joseph, and quite a legend and popular devotion grew up in the area. She was fond of recounting their first meeting. She used to say that Joseph was a messenger from the east bearing great news. He planted his hard dry traveling staff into the stony ground of Britain and it blossomed like the staff of Jesse into a bush whose flowers and fruit shall eventually cover Britain from coast to coast.

Busy days passed until Eleanor noticed it becoming increasingly hard for her to swallow. Over the weeks the complaint grew worse.

She grew weak and couldn't eat and was unable to rise from her bed, and eventually she was unable to drink. The ladies moistened her lips with a cloth with water kept in a goblet near her bed. Eleanor could smell the water in her thirst.

"Dear Lord, please do not scold me for my sins and negligence when I come to you even though I deserve it.

"You have scolded me enough on this side of the divide and I would like to be greeted with something that I shall be able to cherish for eternity.

"And also, Dear Lord, I would like my husband to greet me. It would be more 'balanced' if I were to greet Joseph and Rebecca with my own husband.

"He often used to whisper to me that our love was from eternity—and if that isn't baptism of desire, then what is?"

Eleanor's body was old and wizened. Her hair was wispy gray but still with slight traces of the fiery red which had once crowned her.

Due to dehydration the skin had become sallow and marks lingered if her skin was touched. Only her eyes showed that she still was fully attentive. Her eyes softened as she watched the ladies fussing about her saying prayers for the dying out loud as they worked.

"Oh, I am thirsty! Please turn this thirst into thirst for you— 'like the hart that seeks the running waters, let my heart thirst for you, O Lord.'" Eleanor's lips moved slightly as she muttered these words of the psalm.

The vision in her mind of the spring of cooling water bubbling out of the cleft rock lingered, as the hart slowly turned his head to look at her and she recognized the countenance.

## A RENEWAL OF VOWS

Eleanor looked radiant as her cheek rested against the arm muscles of her husband, now dressed in full armor. Her right hand rested on the crook of his elbow and her left arm was held erect with the horn of plenty in her hand, the symbol of heavenly bounty. She looked almost shyly at the merry throng below, her clothes and hair resplendent in gold and jewelry.

In the full bloom of her youth, she looked more comely than at the first marriage, and her red hair shone in the celestial light.

# ⚘ Epilogue

D emas was old, very old, but his voice was still strong, as he faced the little throng of new arrivals sent by David.

"You stand before the tomb of Joseph. His face was kissed by Jesus. Kiss the tomb of Joseph, who kissed the face of Jesus.

"I know that some of you are here against your natural inclinations. You feel that your abilities could be better spent among the miraculous works that are being achieved in Africa, so why be sent to this swamp at the edge of the world . . . ?

"Let me assure you. . . . You are here because of your generous spirit. Your heart has brought you here, not your head; and you have been faithful to the requests of the Church.

"God is no-one's debtor, and he will reward your obedience with abundant fruit.

"You may be often tempted to think that the work here is too hard and the progress too slow. Yet the nail that is pushed into soft wood comes out easily.

"The nail that you drive into the hard wood of Britain, the nails of Christ crucified, shall remain and because of this hardness will eventually be capable of bearing great weight. Dream, and the reality of God's plans shall multiply them hundreds of times. Work with patience; yours is a work of foundation. Work confidently, and above all with prayer.

"Ladies, here you see the tomb of Eleanor, buried at the feet of Joseph.

"The wooden carving depicts an animal breathing fire with five little offspring, one colored black, one red, one brown, one white and one yellow. The scene seems to depict something that must have happened between them, some private joke that they shared together.

"Our imagination can speculate on anything, but I like to think that the flame coming from her mouth is the breath of the Holy Spirit, which warms the hearts of all peoples, tribes, and nations. Our religion is for all men and women of good will who choose freely to follow the path of the Lord.

"They are buried at the site of a barn that belonged to one of the first Christian families here. The father of the household brought Joseph to Britain in his ship. It was their request that they be buried here. May they rest in peace. Miracles are said to have been worked at these tombs, particularly for people with stiffening of the joints.

"Let us take this as a sign of the Lord's favor and as a sign that the cure of stiffness is an indication of God's willingness to put up with our stubbornness; and to be patient with us until we are docile to his gentle commands.

"If you sometimes feel despondent, then come here and kiss their tombs and ask them to intercede with the Lord for you; that you persevere until the end.

"The courage of Eleanor and Joseph was not the courage of our glorious martyrs, the courage given to some by Christ himself, the courage he gave to my parents: but the slow steady courage of suffering the tedium and dedication of everyday for a lifetime. That too is a martyrdom, a bloodless martyrdom, which is the normal calling for each and everyone of us.

"I hope that you have the courage of a bloody martyr, if called upon by God as his special witness, but in the meantime imitate them in this way of dedicated love.

"Pray for my own father and mother, as I do every day, and pray that we all join them one day in the home of our heavenly Father. Amen."

⌒

Ana tended the grave during her lifetime. She had compiled a book of Eleanor's letters, called "Letters to Ana."

Those ladies, whom she supervised, used to study them carefully and explain their contents to the new ones.

After Ana's death the grave continued to be tended; but religious persecution arose and it became dangerous to visit the grave. All the stone churches were put to other use and the wooden churches near the thoroughfares of the Romans were destroyed. Christianity flourished in secret and spread rapidly in the areas outside Roman influence. The Church became identified with Britain and its way of life. And the number of hermits grew in the remote areas of the country.

Gradually thorn and bramble and stinging weed grew over the grave of Joseph and Eleanor, and the site became inaccessible. The forest came to claim its own.

The village moved to a sunnier spot nearer the docks, and the old houses were abandoned to decay.

Eleanor and Joseph existed only in people's memory.

And so it has been through the ages to the present—a memory like a will-o'-the-wisp on a heavy summer's evening over the marsh of time.

Who knows, whether some day the little light may linger over the spot where, clearing the reeds, there will be a little nest— neat with speckled eggs and a chirping chick?

The nest, resting against the corner of a stone, sticking out of the marsh; nature singing like Calliope to the runes of Joseph.

Joseph
Hic iacit Joseph
Videt qui Deum videt
Sapit qui Deum sapit
Perambulat qui cum Deo perambulat.

(Joseph
Here lies Joseph
He sees who sees God
He tastes who tastes God
He walks who walks with God.)

Shall we make this stone a kissing stone—the voices of the past
locked in its crystals—and shall we surround it by a building
worthy of him, or shall we just leave him to our memories?

After all, why try to put a fence around the wind?

# ✢ Historical Note for Those Not Familiar with European History

Christianity spread through the western part of Britain and eventually reached Ireland, through the efforts of Patrick, a Roman citizen, who was captured as a slave and taken to Ireland, then escaped, and later returned to evangelize the country. Scotland was then converted and northern Britain.

With the invasion of Britain by the Germanic peoples, the saints of Britain sailed against the invasion current and evangelized northern Europe. Eventually, via northern Europe, they saved the Iberian Peninsula from the heresy of Arianism.

Britain and Ireland and the Iberian peninsula eventually brought the Christian faith to the Americas and many other parts of the World.

North Africa became locked in heretical disputes and then largely succumbed to Islam.